PERILOUS JOURNEY TO FREEDOM

A DARING ESCAPE ACROSS THE ALPS

ESCAPING THE REICH
BOOK THREE

MARION KUMMEROW

Perilous Journey to Freedom, Escaping the Reich, Book 3

Marion Kummerow

All Rights Reserved

Copyright © 2025 Marion Kummerow

This book is copyrighted and protected by copyright laws.

No part of this publication may be reproduced or transmitted in any form or by any means, electronic, mechanical, photocopying, recording, or otherwise without prior written permission from the author.

This is a work of fiction. Names, places, characters and incidents are either the product of the author's imagination or are used fictitiously, and any resemblance to any actual persons, living or dead, organizations, events or locales is entirely coincidental.

CHAPTER 1

ST. GALLENKIRCH, MONTAFON, JULY 1943

Felix sat in his father's worn armchair, which still occupied its regular place in the living room. Rays of sunshine fell through the crocheted curtains, painting beautiful patterns on the worn-out wooden floor.

His trusted mountain boots sat on the old table, scuffed and worn from years of use. Replacing them wasn't an option. As long as the war dragged on, every bit of leather and cloth went to the front lines. Civilians were left to patch and pray their old things would hold a little longer.

With practiced movements, he dipped the soft cloth into the tin of leather grease. The smell of beeswax and beef tallow wafted into his nostrils, mingling with the smoke from the fire in the stove. Felix loved the scent, because it indicated he would soon be heading into the mountains again. He simply wasn't meant for a regular life as a farmer.

Carefully, he massaged the grease into the cracks of the worn boot. His fingers felt every seam and every scratch in the brown leather, which turned supple under his care, shining almost as if new. These mountain boots were his faithful companions, without them he would be doomed. When he finished, he examined his work with satisfaction before placing them next to the crackling stove.

His youngest sister, Valentina, often joked that he loved those boots more than he could ever love a woman, and that was the reason he had never married.

The door opened with a creak and Valentina entered, an apron tied around her hips. Together with Felix and their frail mother, she and her five children lived in their parents' house.

"Here you are. I've been looking for you." The resolute woman in her late thirties leaned against the doorframe. Her gaze fell on the freshly polished boots standing next to the stove, and she furrowed her brow. "How much longer do you plan to patch them up?"

Felix gently stroked the leather. "They need to last through one more winter."

Valentina sat on the armrest of his chair. "The next time you cross the border into Switzerland, bring some leather and a last. The old cobbler Pichelhuber can make you new ones. He's discreet."

"I'd have to break them in first, and where would I find the time?"

The practical woman shook her head. "Do you really want to wait until the soles fall off your feet before getting new shoes?"

"We'll see," he said evasively as he closed the tin of leather grease. Breaking in the boots wasn't the real reason he was reluctant to have new ones made. On each of his border crossings, he could only carry a limited amount of goods. Coffee, chocolate and sugar were more important, since he, Valentina and her children, as well as their mother, lived off the sale of the restricted goods in the village. New mountain boots would have to wait.

"I was at the Huber farm earlier, where I ran into Karl. He's stopping by later."

"I thought he was traveling." Felix lifted his head. Karl was his partner, and he'd been doing business with the man for decades. In his youth, Karl had gone on trips himself, until he'd injured his knee in an accident and the steep climbs had become too strenuous for him.

But it turned out that he was a gifted businessman who seemed to attract new customers without any effort. He didn't just work with Felix but was also involved in procuring all sorts of forgeries—these days mainly identification papers.

"You know him. One never really knows where he is or for how long." Valentina shook her head with disapproval.

"That's just the nature of his work. The Gestapo mustn't know too much about what he's up to and who he meets."

"I know." She put her hands on her hips. "I'd prefer if you stayed away from these activities."

"Oh, Vale, I haven't learned anything else besides mountain climbing." As young as five years old, he had accompanied his father on trips across the nearby borders. He knew every path and rock that offered protection from patrols, and had several tricks in his repertoire to mislead potential pursuers.

Over the years, he had built an extensive network of business partners. Farmers, suppliers, and buyers throughout the entire region, on both sides of the border, gladly traded with him because he paid and charged fair prices.

"That's not what I mean, and you know it." She glared at him. "Stop the side business with the Jews."

He scratched the back of his neck. "We've already talked

about it. Smuggling Jews to Switzerland brings in good money."

"With your neck on the line. There's no reason to take the extra risk."

Felix shrugged.

"You know what will happen if you get caught."

"They won't catch me. I'm far too clever. Even if they do, I'll find a way to buy myself out." Every policeman in the region was a good customer of his.

Valentina shook her head. "That won't help you. If you get caught smuggling Jews, you won't go to prison—you'll go straight to the gallows."

"You're exaggerating." Felix stood up. For him, the discussion was over. Since Valentina's husband had been shot by the Nazis shortly after Austria's annexation to the German Reich, she had become very fearful. Her husband had come to the aid of a stranger being beaten in the street—who later turned out to be Jewish.

After checking the cow barn, Felix stepped outside and spotted a familiar head of snow-white hair. It was Karl, his oldest friend—the one he'd shared a school desk with years ago. Even back then, Karl had a way of charming everyone, including their strict teacher, always working some kind of deal or another.

"Hello, Karl! You're back early." Officially, Karl worked as a sales representative for the dairy industry, although he used his trips to the cities to find buyers for smuggled goods and customers for the much riskier part of their business.

"There were rumors the Gestapo was watching my contact, so I changed my plans." Most people saw Karl as nothing more than a charming rogue, but Felix knew better. Karl had a knack for reading people, and spotting danger before it struck.

"Are you staying for dinner?" Felix asked as they walked side by side to the house nestled against the slope.

"Sorry, I have a date in the village."

"I thought the Pichelhuber woman dumped you when she found out about your escapades?"

Karl cast him his most charming smile, the one that melted women left and right—and consistently brought him both love affairs and good business. "She can never stay mad at me for long. She's making Käsespätzle, and I wouldn't miss it for anything."

Pichelhuber's cheese noodle recipe was legendary in the village; even Valentina respected her for it. Felix, though, didn't understand the enthusiasm—he preferred a juicy piece of meat.

"What brings you up here then?"

"A new job. A Jewish family from Lake Constance with two children."

"How old?" Felix glared at his friend. They had made it a rule not to take children because it complicated matters. Children were slow, loud and unpredictable in their behavior. In short, they weren't up to the rigors of fleeing across the mountains. Moreover, parents often made unwise decisions when children were involved.

"Twelve and fourteen. Both strong. Ready to do anything to escape. Their oldest sister was beaten to death before their eyes."

Felix's eyelid twitched. Every day he thought nothing could shock him anymore, and every day he was proven wrong. "All right. When?"

"Next week. The father is a doctor, the mother a housewife. She speaks fluent French. They have relatives in Geneva."

"Valentina wants me to stop the tours with Jews."

Karl nodded. "What's new? She's told me many times, too."

"Her nagging is getting worse."

"She'll come around."

Felix rubbed his earlobe. "I don't know. She's changed since her husband was shot. Constantly afraid of the Gestapo."

"We all are." Karl squinted his eyes at his friend. "Aren't you?"

"Hmm." Felix mulled. "Not really. They're too stupid to catch me."

"Don't be so sure." By now they had reached the house. Karl stopped. "The question is, do you want to continue?"

That was the crux. Felix would gladly stop smuggling Jews because, contrary to what he told everyone, he was well aware that he was risking his life on every trip. But something inside wouldn't let him stop. *We need the money.* He shrugged. "Fine, I'll do this trip. But then we take a break for a few weeks so no one gets suspicious."

"Promise," said Karl. However, Felix knew that neither of them would feel bound by that promise if another refugee in need asked for help.

"I'll find out who's on duty at the border next week." Some of the border guards were corrupt and would look the other way for the right price when Felix showed up with fugitives.

CHAPTER 2

FRANKFURT AM MAIN, JULY 1943

Astrid lived with terror lodged like a stone in her chest. Every time the doorbell rang, her heart stopped. One ring meant danger—maybe *them*. Maybe this time they'd come to tear her life apart. Or worse. She never breathed again until she heard the second and third chime, the secret code whispered through the Jewish community. A quiet promise: *It's safe. It's not the Gestapo.*

But today, the second and third chime never came. Her blood turned to ice. This was it—the moment she'd dreaded for weeks. Her brothers weren't home. Her Aryan mother wasn't either. Her father was in the bathroom, the scrape of his razor muffled behind the closed door.

It was *she* who had to answer.

Heavy boots thundered up the stairs.

Panic took over. She lunged for the breakfast table, snatching the butter, the bread, the jar of jam and shoved it all under the heavy cabinet just as the footsteps reached the landing.

Seconds later, someone hammered against the apartment door. Astrid took a deep breath and called out: "I'm coming!" to make the Gestapo stop their angry pounding before the door, already badly damaged from their last visit, burst open.

When she pulled on the handle, an officer shoved her aside and stepped into the living room, which doubled as her parents' bedroom since the family of five had been forced to move into the dilapidated two-room apartment. Two more officers followed on the heels of the intruder.

"My father—" She stopped mid-sentence as her father emerged from the tiny bathroom at that very moment. Shaving cream clung to one earlobe and his shirt was buttoned up wrong.

He flinched at the sight of the three uniformed men. Protectively, he positioned himself between Astrid and the police officers—there was nothing else he could do. While the two subordinates searched the apartment for illegal supplies —these days, even the possession of legally purchased bread in a Jewish household could be considered a crime if the Gestapo was in a bad mood—their leader planted himself wide-legged in front of them.

"Name?" he asked mockingly, despite knowing perfectly well who lived here. After all, it wasn't the first time he'd tormented the Hambach family.

"Alfred Israel Hambach," her father answered.

"A filthy Jew, then." The Scharführer's face twisted in disgust as he spat in her father's face.

Astrid admired her father's self-control: He didn't move a muscle and resisted the temptation to wipe the disgusting spittle from his face, not wanting to give the Scharführer a reason to beat him. A former neighbor had ended up in the hospital after a house search and, a few weeks later, in a concentration camp. Once the Gestapo had it in for you, even the tiniest real or perceived offense could be punished by death.

To avoid making any mistakes, Astrid stood stock-still, barely daring to breathe. Dishes clattered in the kitchen. She hoped they wouldn't shatter one of the four plates their five-person household owned.

One of the men returned to the living room with a bag of flour. "Look what I found!"

"These greedy Jews really stop at nothing." The Scharführer shook his head with disgust before turning toward Astrid: "Don't you know that hoarding supplies is illegal?"

"My mother bought the flour. She's Aryan."

"She's a shameless Jewish whore!"

Astrid bit her tongue; under no circumstances was she allowed to contradict the enraged man. Her restraint, however, seemed to anger him even more.

"Say that your mother is a shameless Jewish whore!" he shouted at her.

"My mother is," Astrid whispered, her gaze fixed on the Scharführer's mocking smirk, "a wonderful woman."

The next moment, a punch struck her jaw and hurled her to the floor. She tasted blood. Tears of pain and rage burned in her eyes. The Scharführer paid her no further attention and turned to his subordinate. This dismissal felt like another blow. To him, she was nothing more than a pesky insect that could be forgotten once crushed in a corner.

The Scharführer took the flour bag and dumped its entire contents onto the carpet. Like gray snow, the flour—for which Mother had queued for hours—trickled to the ground, mixing with the dirt from the Gestapo's boots. Probably little to nothing could be salvaged.

Astrid swallowed repeatedly at the sight. Next came the potatoes she had peeled for dinner. Like a small child, the

Scharführer beamed with joy as he crushed the meal for five people beneath his heavy boots. She watched in disbelief, hoping the Gestapo at least wouldn't find the hidden supplies under the cabinets and behind the stove. Otherwise, the family would have to go hungry during the remainder of the month.

"Tsk. It's unbelievable how dirty it is in here," said the Scharführer as he turned around himself to survey his work. His gaze fell on Astrid. So much for hoping he'd forgotten about her. "Get up, you lazy pig. Why aren't you at work?"

"I... I work the late shift this week." She was barely able to control the trembling in her limbs.

"Excuses, nothing but excuses. Work-shy vermin. First starting the war and then wanting to watch with pleasure as Germany is destroyed. But not with us. He who laughs last laughs best, and that will be the German master race."

By the time Astrid rose to her feet, the Scharführer had lost interest in humiliating her and strode over to the bookshelf. He randomly pulled out a book, flipped through its pages and threw it behind him. With a quick sidestep, Astrid moved out of the line of fire. The book landed with a dull thud on top of the flour and squashed potatoes. Astrid choked at the sight. It was an all-too-fitting symbol of the Nazis' cultural barbarism.

Spurred on by their superior's example, the other two officers reached peak performance. They tore pictures from the walls, slashed the upholstery of the armchairs, dumped the contents of drawers and trampled on them. Mother's carefully guarded sewing supplies were scattered across the carpet, so that it would take days to pick up the countless pins.

Astrid watched their actions with helpless rage. Any protest would have further fueled the men's destructive fury and prolonged the senseless rampage. Instead, she sought her father's gaze and hoped the Gestapo would soon lose interest and look for other victims.

But it wasn't over yet. One of the men paused briefly, looking at a family photo before tearing it to pieces. The scraps floated to the floor, joining the mess of flour, squashed potatoes, pins and all sorts of other things. The image of scattered ashes after a fire crossed Astrid's mind. Silently, she implored the patron saint against fire hazards with the old saying: "Saint Florian, spare my house, kindle others."

Inwardly, she despised herself, because the years under the Nazi yoke had turned her into a cold-hearted being who cared only about herself and her family. The terrible experiences had numbed her to the suffering happening to people around her. These days she hardly felt compassion, when yet another acquaintance was arrested or killed.

Shame burned through her because her first thought was always the same, a quiet relief that she had been spared. The second thought was even worse. It was the hope that the dead had left something behind, a pair of knee socks or a mended blouse, anything to supplement her own clothing, which was tattered beyond recognition, since Jews weren't entitled to clothing ration cards.

The other Gestapo officer appeared with an electric stove in his hand. Grinning, he said, "We're confiscating this thing."

"Please, don't. It's our only way to cook," her father pleaded.

"You'll have to get used to eating cold potatoes, you Jewish swine," said the Scharführer, taking the electric stove and signaling his men to leave.

Finally, the search ended. The three uniformed men left the apartment, slamming the door behind them with a finality that sent a shiver down Astrid's spine. She waited until she heard the thunder of their footsteps in the apartment one floor above, before she finally felt safe again. Saint Florian had heard her prayers: The Gestapo was setting someone else's house on fire.

The relief was short-lived. After a glance at the chaos in the living room, Astrid threw herself into her father's arms, overwhelmed by despair.

"We survived, my darling. They're gone." Father kept stroking her back in a soothing manner, although she could feel how badly his hand was shaking.

"We've had luck in our misfortune. The Gestapo didn't find our hidden supplies," she murmured.

"And we're both still here to tell the tale." He pulled away from her. "We should clean up, or your mother will have a heart attack once she comes home from shopping."

"He took the electric stove," Astrid sobbed. "How are we supposed to cook our meals?" Without the electric stove, they would surely starve. They couldn't eat raw potatoes, which, besides bread, were practically their only food.

"We'll figure something out. First thing tomorrow morning, I'll visit the Jewish community's lending center and ask if they can loan us a replacement," Father suggested.

"Do that." Astrid fetched a dustpan and broom. Her father's suggestion was hopeless; the Jewish lending center didn't deserve the name, as their stock was basically non-existent. While sweeping up, she had an idea and promptly devised a plan to retrieve the precious electric stove so the family wouldn't have to starve. As a precaution, she didn't tell her father, who surely would have tried to talk her out of it.

Astrid moved through the rest of the day like a ghost, not quite able to shake off the lingering terror from the Gestapo's raid. Her father didn't notice how quiet she was. When it was time, she pulled on her worn coat and slipped outside, walking the familiar path to the factory where she worked. Every step she took tightened her resolve.

Her work shift ended at midnight. It was the perfect time for Astrid's plan. Instead of heading home, she directed her steps toward the warehouses where the goods confiscated by the Gestapo were stored.

As soon as she deviated from the direct route home, she was putting her life in danger. Her permission to be out on the street after the curfew for Jews applied solely to the direct route from the factory to her apartment, while the warehouses with the looted items lay in the opposite direction. The closer she got to the junction, the stronger the queasy feeling in her stomach became, until she was about to throw up.

Once she reached the intersection, she carefully peered in all directions. No one was in sight, even the moon was hiding behind a cloud. Anxiously, she felt for the bent hairpin and the flashlight in her jacket pocket. She took both and pushed them deep into the pockets of her skirt.

Then she took off her jacket with the telltale yellow star and draped it over her shoulders, the sleeves loosely knotted in front. With her light brown hair and pert nose, she didn't match the image of the Jewish race the Nazis had defined in supposedly scientific publications. This fact had often worked to her advantage, therefore she hoped not to be stopped and asked for her papers—after all, Aryans were allowed to walk freely on the streets at any time of day or night.

A slight discomfort remained, causing goosebumps on her arms. If she were caught concealing the yellow star, she risked immediate arrest.

Drenched in sweat, she reached the warehouse grounds on the outskirts of the city. Everything was quiet and deserted; no light and no soul in sight. On this night, not even the constant hum of bomber squadrons or the dull thudding of anti-aircraft guns disrupted the silence.

Cautiously looking in all directions, Astrid crept to the

entrance gate, which was secured with a padlock. Years ago, her brothers had taught her how to pick the pantry lock without leaving a trace—back when the family had lived in modest prosperity in a beautiful apartment in Frankfurt-Höchst.

She had learned the trick, back when life had still felt safe. After her perpetually hungry brothers had raided the chocolate meant for their father's birthday cake, her mother had started locking up the sweets. Astrid smiled faintly at the memory. She had spent weeks teaching herself how to pick that pantry lock—only to be caught by her mother on her very first stealing mission and given a stern lecture. Years later she'd learned it wasn't picking the lock that had given her away, but the smear of chocolate on her mouth.

Her guilty conscience stirred. Back then, she had solemnly promised her mother never to break in anywhere again. But today was different: The Gestapo had stolen Astrid's family's electric stove, and she was merely taking back what rightfully belonged to them.

Another shiver raced through her body from head to toe. If she got caught, the consequences would be severe. She banished the thought, because she had to focus. After making sure once more that there wasn't a single soul in sight, she retrieved the hairpin from her skirt pocket.

During her work shift, she had shaped one end into a hook. Using the moonlight to guide her, she inserted the straight end into the lock until a strange sound froze her hand mid-action. Holding her breath, she remained motionless, pressing herself against the gate. A few seconds later, a cat sprang from the wall. Its eyes glowed yellow in the darkness, as it seemed to stare reproachfully at Astrid. Unable to move, Astrid stared back. Shortly after, the cat turned its head and ran away.

Phew, that was a close call. Astrid wiped the sweat from her forehead. As she struggled to push the hairpin into the keyhole a second time, her hands were shaking so badly that she kept missing it.

Despondent, she lowered her arm and was about to slink away when her inner fighting spirit spoke up in the voice of one of her brothers: *You're not going to give up, are you? Baby!*

That was exactly what she had intended to do. Even though her brother wasn't really taunting her, she would never show weakness in front of him—or his voice in her head. Defiance flowed through her. She closed her eyes, took a deep breath, and imagined herself effortlessly and confidently inserting the hairpin. In her mind, she rehearsed each motion until she was sure it would work.

Then she turned back to the lock, inserted the hairpin in one swift movement until she felt resistance. Carefully, she twisted the pin just a bit, as if it were the key. This was the most difficult part, because one had to apply enough pressure to put tension on the mechanism without overturning it.

While holding the straight end of the hairpin with one hand, she inserted the bent end into the upper opening of the lock with the other one. Hidden inside were the pins she had to overturn one by one. Feeling her way forward with utmost care, while keeping one ear attentive to her surroundings, she worked diligently until the first pin clicked. Her nervousness vanished. The first pin was always the hardest one; once you managed that, the rest was child's play.

With careful movements, her fingers produced click after click. Despite the rising euphoria, she couldn't allow herself to be distracted, since the tension inside the mechanism had to remain constant. If she decreased the pressure or released it completely due to a scare, all the pins she had already been opened would lock again, and she would have to start over.

Finally, a solid click sounded when the last pin sprung open. Astrid allowed herself a small grin, while she continued to turn the hairpin until the lock sprang open with a metallic sound. In the night's silence, it seemed louder to her than a bomb strike, making her worried that it must have been audible for kilometers around.

As a precaution, she listened for a few seconds before letting lock and hairpin slide into her pocket. Then she opened the gate a crack and slipped inside. There was no time to waste. At any moment a patrol could come by and notice the missing lock. But she didn't want to leave the lock hanging and risk being shut inside.

The warehouse smelled of musty furniture, misery, and fear. After pulling the iron gate closed behind her, she switched on the flashlight and felt her way forward in its dim beam, her heart hammering viciously against her ribs.

To the right and left of the narrow central aisle stood piled furniture, boxes, and household items. She recognized her neighbors' plundered chandelier. A floor lamp looked familiar, too. Next to it was a table with electrical appliances, containing everything from hair dryers to toasters, vacuum cleaners, and electric irons. But not their electric stove.

So she moved on to the next table, which was stacked with metallic things: pots, cups, colanders, cutlery, and at the very back, their electric stove, easily recognizable by the nick on one side.

Astrid would have loved to take other useful things the Nazis had stolen from the Jews, but she wanted to avoid anyone noticing the loss. Besides, she had limited space. She took off her neck scarf, wrapped the electric stove in it and stowed it in her shoulder bag beneath her dirty work smock that she had brought along specifically for this purpose.

In the process, she bumped against a stack of dishes with her elbow. A cup fell to the floor and shattered. The noise echoed in her ears like a thunderclap. Outside, a dog barked.

Astrid immediately extinguished the flashlight, waiting

motionless in the darkness. Seconds stretched into eternities. Finally, the dog fell silent. Nobody else seemed to have noticed. After a few minutes she dared to risk turning the flashlight on. She collected the shards and pushed them under a pile of curtains. Then she walked to the gate, slipped through, hung the padlock and raced home as fast as she could manage.

Once she had closed the apartment door behind her, she finally took a deep breath of relief. She had done it. Her family wouldn't have to starve.

CHAPTER 3

A MOUNTAIN VILLAGE IN MONTAFON, JULY 1943

High up on the slope, Bärbel Egger spotted her grandmother's house. Out of breath after the vigorous two-hour climb from the bus stop in the town of Sankt Gallenkirch, she paused. Sweat dripped from her forehead as she shielded her eyes against the blazing sun. Regardless, she didn't take off her thick sweater, since up here in the Alps, at over 1400 meters, the temperature in the shade never really warmed.

Gasping for breath, she set down her heavy suitcase, enjoying the magnificent view of the majestic mountain peaks with their glittering, snow-covered tips. The contrast was stark against the black forests below the tree line and the lush green meadows in the valley. Cool mountain air brushed against her heated cheeks, gradually easing her tension.

The scent of pine trees and grass hung in the air. Memories of happy childhood days flooded her brain. Together with her brothers Achim and Karsten she had spent numerous carefree holidays at their grandparents' home. In summer, they had romped all day in the meadows or played smugglers and customs officers in the forest. In winter, they had raced down the slopes on skis—and laboriously climbed back up. She had enjoyed every single day. But those happy time were long gone.

Once again, Bärbel picked up her suitcase and marched uphill for another hour until she stood in front of the ancient wooden house at the edge of the small mountain village of Gargellen. For a few minutes she lingered at the garden gate until her pulse normalized. Then she tackled the last few steps and knocked on the door.

Anxious seconds passed during which nothing stirred. Just as Bärbel feared her grandmother might not be home, finally footsteps sounded. The door creaked open, and her grandmother's wrinkled face appeared. "Bärbel! What are you doing here? Has something happened?"

"May I come in?" She hugged her grandmother tight.

"Of course. I'll make us some hot cocoa, then you can tell me everything." The sprightly eighty-year-old led the way into the kitchen, where the wood stove spread cozy warmth.

"You have cocoa?" In the city of Innsbruck, where Bärbel studied medicine, cocoa had become a scarce commodity, basically unavailable for years.

"Felix Wallner sold me a package two months ago." Grandmother winked at her.

"He's still going to Switzerland? I thought the Nazis had closed the border."

"They have, but locals still know the old secret paths. Especially Felix, he knows every stone in the region. But now tell me, what brings you here? Shouldn't you be at the university studying?"

"Yes and no," Bärbel hedged. She had left Innsbruck in a hurry, stuffing only the most important things into her suitcase. About halfway through her journey, she had decided to temporarily hide at her grandmother's house.

At that moment, the milk in the pot started to bubble. Grandmother moved the pot off the burner and stirred in cocoa powder until a wonderful aroma filled the room. Suddenly Bärbel's future looked much brighter.

Her grandmother filled two mugs and prepared to carry them into the parlor, but Bärbel beat her to it. "Let me do that, please."

At the large table, where ten or more people had used to sit, Bärbel felt lost. She wrapped her hands around the hot mug, taking cautious sips of cocoa and using the delay to organize her thoughts. During the march uphill, she had been too anxious to think clearly and still didn't know what or how much to tell her grandmother.

"So, why are you here?" Grandmother's body might have become hunched over the decades, but her mind remained razor-sharp.

"I had to disappear." Bärbel groaned as she replayed the events of the past few months in her mind's eye. "I might be on a wanted list by the Gestapo."

Grandmother examined her thoroughly. "Both your brothers died in the war, your father is in prison for criticizing the regime. Shall I lose you too?"

"I'm sorry." Guilt crept through her limbs, all but paralyzing her. Bärbel didn't want to lie to her grandmother, so she decided to tell the truth. "Have you heard of the White Rose?"

A nod was the answer. "It was big news in the papers. Some students in Munich wrote heretical leaflets. They were caught when they scattered their pamphlets in the atrium of the university."

"...and were executed for their actions," Bärbel added. Whenever she thought about it, a lump formed in her throat.

"One member of the White Rose, Christoph Probst, was a fellow student of mine."

"That alone isn't enough reason to arrest you. And why now? The members of the White Rose were executed months ago."

Bärbel shrugged, taking another sip of her cocoa while carefully choosing her words. "We belonged to the same circle of friends." Her grandmother's piercing gaze prompted her to give more details. "After Christoph's arrest, the rest of our group continued the resistance against the regime. We created and distributed leaflets. Last week, almost everyone in the group was arrested. I was lucky because I was doing an internship at a military hospital. Someone warned me not to return to Innsbruck. I had to disappear."

"Thus you came to me." Grandmother shook her head.

"I couldn't think of anyone else. They will surely look for me at my mother's place."

"Does anyone know you were planning to come here?"

"No. Nobody." Bärbel blew on her cocoa, watching as the patterns formed on the surface. With a sad sigh, she added, "I didn't even tell Mutti."

"How did you get here?"

Bärbel tucked a strand of hair behind her ear. "By bus to Sankt Gallenkirch, from there I marched up on foot."

Grandmother snorted. "Then half of Montafon has seen you. I hope at least you didn't tell anyone who you are?"

"No, I didn't. I didn't encounter a single person on my way up."

"Oh, little Bärbel. News travels fast in this remote area." Grandmother stroked her cheek. "For now, you can certainly stay with me. But we must be careful. Not all villagers are trustworthy; actually quite a few are in cahoots with the Nazis."

"Thank you so much. I definitely don't want to get you into trouble, Grandma. But I didn't know where else to go."

Grandmother stood up and paced around. She stopped at the window with her back to Bärbel and looked out, as if the answer lay hidden somewhere in the mountains. Eventually, Bärbel stepped beside her.

Beneath the living room window lay the terrace. From there, a path led to the shelter where the firewood was stored. Next to it stood the splitting block, small wood scraps from splitting scattered on the earth. About a five-minute walk diagonally up the slope was the pasture for the milk cow and some goats. Just beyond it began the forest. The village below them could only be seen from the kitchen window on the other side of the house.

"Of course you'll stay. At least for now," Grandmother said energetically, taking Bärbel's hand in hers. "I wouldn't be much of a grandmother if I sent my granddaughter away."

"Thank you, Grandma." A wave of relief warmed Bärbel from within. She could always count on her grandmother.

"My house is far enough from the village that you can stay here undetected. Regardless, we need to take some precautions."

"Maybe the Gestapo isn't even looking for me." Deep in her heart, Bärbel hoped she might soon return to the university in Innsbruck, although she didn't actually believe it to be possible. Since Austria's annexation, life had become complicated, at least for those who didn't wholeheartedly support the Nazi rule.

"Don't count on it too much. From what we know, the Gestapo wants to arrest you." Grandmother smoothed her long, dark green linen dress. "We need to work on a strategy."

Bärbel seemed to float in the air. Her grandmother had just taken a heavy burden off her shoulders. She was no longer alone in this, she had an ally she could rely on one hundred percent.

"That sounds good." Bärbel's stomach growled in agreement.

Smiling, her grandmother asked, "Are you hungry, little Bärbel?"

"Hungry as a bear. I haven't eaten since yesterday evening, because I left at the crack of dawn today."

"Did you bring food ration cards?"

"Yes, they're in my suitcase."

"That's good." In the next second, Grandmother bit her lip. "We can't use them, or else I'd have to register you in the village."

"And then the Gestapo will find out I'm here." Bärbel tucked a strand of hair behind her ear.

"Well, we'll manage somehow. I don't get ration cards for myself either, because I'm classified as self-sufficient."

"I really don't want to cause you any trouble." Bärbel was on the verge of suggesting to her grandmother that she would leave the next day.

"You're not, my dear. I'll think of something. We can always slaughter a chicken."

"Aren't they registered?"

"Yes." The mischievous grin made Grandmother look like a young woman. "But these careless chickens tend to escape and get lost in the forest, where the fox gets them."

"Please don't get yourself into trouble because of me."

Grandmother put her arm around Bärbel's shoulders. "If not for you, then for whom? Family must stick together."

"Thank you, Grandma." Bärbel was moved to tears.

"It's the least I can do. And now I'll cook us a hearty stew. You've gotten terribly thin since your last visit."

That was true. The food supply in the city was nowhere

near as abundant as in the countryside. "I'll take my things to the room in the meantime."

"Do that, my dear."

While her grandmother cooked dinner, Bärbel climbed upstairs to the chamber she had used to share with her two brothers during her school holiday stays.

A lump formed in her throat. Both of them had been drafted into the Wehrmacht soon after the war began and had died heroic deaths for Führer and Fatherland. She clenched her fists. Neither of them had been asked whether they wanted to go into battle for Hitler; otherwise, they would have refused.

Now they were dead. Her mother hadn't even received their bodies for a dignified burial. Achim had been hastily buried by his comrades in the dirt of the battlefield; a hand grenade had left nothing worth burying of Karsten.

I'm sorry, Mutti. I'll do everything so you won't lose your daughter too.

CHAPTER 4

SANKT GALLENKIRCH, AUGUST 1943

Felix fed the wood stove with pages torn from his notebook. Names, dates, and orders—all information better unknown. Ever since he was a young lad, his father had impressed upon him the importance of immediately destroying any evidence of forbidden business once the deal was done.

After Austria's annexation into the German Reich, this habit had become crucial for survival. When he heard footsteps behind him, he flinched, quickly tossing the last scraps of paper into the fire and closing the hatch before turning around. "Oh, it's you, Vale."

"Everything burned?" His sister glanced meaningfully at the stove.

"Yes. Do you need the stove for cooking?"

"No."

Felix sensed trouble, fearing a lecture about the dangers of his business. "If you've come to lecture me—"

She cut him off. "I haven't. I have news from the village."

He knew his sister well enough to hear the dark undertone in her voice. Frowning, he asked, "What happened?"

"One of your colleagues betrayed two Jews from Graz. He abandoned them at St. Antönier mountain pass, where they promptly ran into the border guards."

His face darkened. He slammed his fist against the wall, making the dishes in the cabinet rattle. "What a cowardly bastard! Do you know who it was?"

Valentina placed a calming hand on his arm. "Don't get so worked up, it'll only cause you trouble. I'm sure you'll find out soon enough."

"You bet I will! I'll ask around." Felix already had someone in mind.

"This afternoon we need to walk down to the village. The mayor has ordered every resident to the marketplace to witness the public execution of the Jews."

"Those damn filthy pigs!" This time Felix pounded his fist on the table, which groaned under the impact.

Valentina glared at him. "Keep your temper in check, or you'll land us in hot water. The Gestapo has their eye on you anyway. They've long suspected that you're smuggling more than just coffee and sugar across the border."

Felix rubbed his aching hand. It was a well-kept secret in the village that he guided paying customers safely across the mountains into Switzerland. This business was far more lucrative than trafficking scarce goods, yet it was also significantly riskier. If he was caught, a night in the cell wouldn't be the end of it.

"Just another year or two, then I can pay off the mortgage on our parents' house, buy the neighbor's pastures, and retire." He'd been telling this dream to his sister for a long time, but something always came up: the expensive roof repair, their mother's fall resulting in a broken hip and a long hospital stay, the annexation and shortly after, the outbreak of war.

If he was honest with himself, these events were just excuses. Deep in his heart, he wasn't ready to give up the mountain crossings to lead a quiet life as a farmer. He simply wasn't cut out for staying at home day in and day out, holding down a regular job.

"At least stop smuggling Jews. It'll be the death of you," Valentina pleaded.

"And what are we supposed to live on? Life has gotten incredibly expensive since the Nazis took over." He looked at his sister with narrowed eyes. Although she often acted like his mother, she was his closest ally.

Before she had married and raised five children, she had often crossed the border herself. She knew the mountains just as well as Felix did. Moreover, she was as nimble and sure-footed as an ibex. Many men could learn a thing or two from her.

Valentina's shoulders slumped. A hint of melancholy crossed her usually tomboyish face. "We'll manage somehow. I can clean houses in the village."

"Oh, really? And who'll take care of the household and our mother while you're working?" His voice sounded sharper than intended. "Who'll sell the goods I organize? Who'll maintain contact with our customers? Who'll listen to the village women for the latest rumors? Who'll find out which goods are in shortest supply?"

She shrugged.

"I need you by my side, Vale. If you're polishing some bigwig's golden faucets, our business won't run smoothly. Soon, we'll have nothing to eat."

"We can live off our reserves for a while." A stubborn look appeared on her face. "Please. Just until the dust settles on the last incident."

Involuntarily, he winced. The memory of his last trip sat like a deep thorn in his soul. It had been damned close. Someone had given the dirt on him to the Gestapo, resulting in his near-arrest, while he was guiding a Jewish family with their two adolescent sons across the border.

Thank God the Gestapo henchmen were out-of-town oafs who didn't know the region well. Felix's knowledge of hidden mountain paths had saved him and the family, allowing them to escape by a hair's breadth. Unlike his traitorous colleague, whose name he was adamant about discovering, he had never lost any of his charges.

After a long moment of silence, Felix sighed, not wanting to worry his sister more than necessary. She was already in constant concern since her sixteen-year-old twin sons had been conscripted to serve as anti-aircraft helpers in Innsbruck. "All right. I won't take any refugees across the border for a while. But the family business with coffee and butter has to continue."

"Thank you." Relief pulled up the corners of her mouth.

"I'll go get some wood. I found a fallen tree further up toward Gargellen."

Valentina pursed her lips. "Have you already forgotten that we've been summoned to the village?"

Felix hadn't forgotten. The thought of the impending execution made him nauseous, and he had no intention of attending the gruesome spectacle. "I'll be back long before then."

His sister wasn't fooled. "Absolutely not. You're just trying to get out."

"So what if I am? No one will notice." He rubbed his neck. "Otherwise, just say I'm on a tour."

"You were playing Skat in the pub until late last night." She put her hands on her hips. "The entire village knows you're at home. If you don't show up, questions will be asked."

Felix cursed beneath his breath. As usual, his sister was right. "If it must be."

"It definitely must. You don't want to be suspected of being a friend to Jews."

Valentina untied her apron and hung it on the hook beside the kitchen door. "The announcement was clear: Every resident must attend. The elderly, the sick, the children. Even Mother."

"Do you really want to drag our mother down to the village?" The Wallner farm lay a good half-hour walk above the village. At nearly eighty years old, Resi Wallner spent most of her time knitting in the rocking chair in her room. Since she had broken her hip, walking had become very strenuous for her.

"It doesn't matter whether I want to or not." Valentina's shoulders sagged, and she suddenly looked very old. Since her husband had died and the twins had been forcibly conscripted to Innsbruck, she carried the main burden of work on the farm.

"I'll see if the blacksmith will lend us his horse for the journey home, so she won't have to walk uphill." Felix rubbed his nose.

"That would be a relief. I'll tell her to get dressed."

Felix grinned. No matter how old and frail his mother had become, she wouldn't visit the village without being properly dressed up.

"We need to leave after lunch," said Valentina before climbing the stairs to her mother's room.

When they arrived at the marketplace in the afternoon, it was already full, partly with curious onlookers, partly with people who, like Felix himself, would rather be anywhere else. On the long side of the square, a hastily constructed wooden platform had been built. The gallows placed upon it pointed skyward like a warning finger. Without meaning to, Felix pulled his jacket tighter around himself.

In the crowd, he spotted his business partner and friend Karl, who distributed most of the smuggled goods to the larger cities. Their eyes met briefly, without greeting each other. The locals knew that Karl and Felix had been friends since elementary school, but the new German authorities should be left believing they had no current business relationship.

Amid the murmurs of the crowd, two young women were led onto the platform. They must have been pretty before their faces had been disfigured by beatings and their hair shaved off. Torn, blood-stained dresses hung in tatters on their bodies.

Felix considered himself hardened, yet he had to turn his head aside, because the pitiful sight made bile rise in his throat. In doing so, his gaze met that of one of the women for the briefest moment. The despair in her dark eyes sent a dagger deep into his heart. Inside his jacket pockets, he clenched his fists tight, until his fingernails dug painfully into his palms. He despised the Nazis from the depths of his soul, especially in this moment, during the public display of their perfidious power.

The mayor, a short, pudgy man with thinning hair, stepped forward and gave a long speech about the necessity of civic courage. With a raised voice, he admonished those present to immediately report any suspicious occurrences.

He was flanked by the local village policemen. To his right stood Fritz, who had gone to school with Felix and Karl and had since worked his way up to local police chief and NSDAP leader. To the left of the mayor stood Oberführer Schmitt, a Nazi party loyalist if there ever was one. He was probably the only one among the locals who had internalized the racial ideology and considered the Jews especially as vermin that had to be exterminated.

When the mayor finished his speech, the German Gestapo chief took over. Felix couldn't stand the tall man with cold eyes and military-style cropped hair. One had to be wary of him. The Gestapo chief's voice bellowed across the square as he launched into one of his usual hate tirades.

"The Jewish race has always been masters of disguise. They adopt any political conviction that benefits them. The Jews are behind Bolshevism, behind Stalin, behind Churchill, and also behind Roosevelt. They throw themselves at the mercy of any of our enemies and have driven us into this war."

The Gestapo chief worked himself into a rage, inciting against the Jews with a red face. "The goal of these perfidious efforts is Jewish world domination. But not with us!" With a sweeping gesture, he included the gathered villagers. "We belong to the master race! We will win this war! As surely as I stand here, we will destroy every single member of the devious Jewish race!"

Since he couldn't endure the sight of the tormented women any longer, Felix let his gaze sweep over the assembled village community. As far as he saw, everyone had come—whether out of enthusiasm, sense of duty, or fear of consequences, he wasn't sure.

Even old carpenter Brandner had made the difficult journey to the marketplace. He stood unsteadily leaning on his cane and his daughter-in-law's arm. Ever since Felix was a boy, the old man had sat on the bench in front of his workshop chatting with customers, while his now-fallen son and recently his grandson were running the business. His wrinkled face revealed no emotion. Felix wouldn't have been surprised if the old, half-blind and deaf man had no idea what was happening on the wooden stage. He would have gladly traded places with him to avoid experiencing the spectacle with all his senses.

At the end of the speech, the Gestapo officers, all of them Germans, as well as the village policemen applauded frenetically. The locals joined in, much more hesitantly. Even Felix took his hands out of his pockets and clapped them together. He hated himself for applauding and was tempted to spit on the ground in order to get rid of the stale taste in his mouth.

Shortly after, a hoarse murmur rippled through the crowd, drawing Felix' attention to the platform. Their hands tied behind their backs, the two women were led to the gallows, where two ropes dangled side by side. The executioner pushed them onto the stools beneath the ropes.

Felix tried to direct his gaze somewhere between the two women so that no one could denounce him for a lack of enthusiasm, yet he didn't have to watch the horrible show. But as if by an invisible magnet, his eyes were drawn to one of the women.

The naked horror, the deep despair, and the wistfulness in her eyes hit him like a punch to the stomach. Involuntarily, he doubled over, until an elbow jabbed his side.

"Don't let yourself go like that," Valentina hissed.

He loved his sister with all his heart, although sometimes —like right now—her maternal manner drove him to white-hot rage. At fifty-five years old, he didn't need admonitions from her. Grinding his teeth, he straightened his spine and forced himself to stand straight, staring at the space between the condemned women, while his mind escaped to his beloved mountains. Up there, the air was clear and thin, no man-made laws applied, and nature ruled over life and death.

Distracted by his memories of sun-drenched peaks and rocky ridges, he didn't witness how the stools were kicked away and the women dangled on the rope until life had drained from them. Another elbow jab brought him back to the present.

"It's over. We are leaving," said Valentina in a strained voice, visibly affected by the spectacle.

"I'm staying in the village to ask around."

"Are you completely insane?" Her voice was a sharp whisper. "I thought you wanted to keep a low profile."

"I need to find out who was the cowardly pig that abandoned the women to save his own miserable life," Felix muttered between clenched teeth.

"You're practically begging for trouble!" Valentina glared at him, her lips pressed into a thin line. He stared back, just as unyielding.

"Good Lord, stubborn as a mule!" With these words, she turned around, taking her mother's arm. Then she said, much louder: "Felix is going to the pub. Probably to celebrate this act of justice with the others."

Immediately his anger vanished. Even when she was angry with him, she always had his back.

CHAPTER 5

FRANKFURT, AUGUST 1943

Astrid stood on the platform of the streetcar rattling through the city. Normally, she hated standing outside, especially when it rained. Today was different. The evening was mild, the breeze cool against her skin as it played with her curls and whispered around her ears. In the west, the evening sky turned fiery red as the sun sank below the horizon.

After glancing at the empty sky, she breathed a sigh of relief. The English bombers seemed to be targeting another city tonight. She had long given up worrying about the future or mourning the past; in the fourth year of the war, Astrid lived exclusively in the present. She didn't dare plan more than two or three days ahead, since she could never be certain she'd still be alive by then.

At the next stop, a man in an SS uniform stepped onto the platform. Before entering the compartment, he scrutinized the passengers. She recognized the burly man with blond hair and protruding ears. During the last house search, he had punched her in the jaw and spat on her father after ransacking their apartment, spilling their precious flour, and crushing their last potatoes under his boots. At least she had managed to get her family's stolen electric oven back.

An unbridled hatred of the Nazis' harassment welled up inside her, and for a moment, she dreamed of pummeling the repulsive man with her fists. She resisted the urge to cover the yellow star on her breast with her arm and instead turned away from the SS man as inconspicuously as possible, but it was too late.

He had already spotted the star and barked at her: "Get off the tram, you filthy Jewish swine!"

Astrid flinched. Mustering her inner calm, she answered: "I'm coming from work. I have a travel permit."

"I couldn't care less." The officer took a step toward her, a smirk on his face. "I don't want to ride in the same tram as Jewish scum. So get lost, or I'll drag you off by your hair!"

Any objection would just provoke him further. Astrid didn't want to risk being beaten, arrested, or murdered on the spot. Thus, she had no choice but to step off the platform. Standing on the sidewalk, she watched as the tram rattled away. At this hour, the next tram on her line would arrive in twenty minutes—if it was on time.

Annoyed with herself, Astrid tilted her head back and buried her hands in the pockets of her only coat, which was far too warm for the season. If she had paid better attention to her surroundings, instead of admiring the sunset, she wouldn't be standing on the sidewalk waiting for the next tram.

Her fingers fumbled for her wallet, until suddenly her annoyance gave way to despair. The wallet contained exactly ten pfennigs, not enough to buy another ticket. With her luck today, she didn't want to count on finding a kind-hearted conductor who would let her board using the old ticket.

"Just great," she muttered, setting off on foot for the long journey home.

She had been walking for about half an hour and darkness had settled over the city, when she passed a blackberry hedge and stopped. After looking carefully in all directions, she picked a handful of leaves and fished out a piece of paper from her handbag, in which she rolled the blackberry leaves into a cigarette, immediately lighting it.

A friend had given her the tip about blackberry leaves, because as a woman and a Jew, Astrid had long been denied tobacco ration cards. After an adjustment period, the blackberry substitute tasted surprisingly good and suppressed the constant feeling of hunger, just like real cigarettes did.

Possession of tobacco carried nothing less than the death penalty. Not officially, but once a Jew was arrested, their chances of survival diminished with each day spent in custody.

During the past two years, countless acquaintances and friends of Astrid had been arrested; just a handful had been released again. Some had been "suicided," allegedly hanging themselves in their cells, while others had been taken to a concentration camp and shot during transport in a staged escape attempt.

Then there was a third group of detainees: those who were deported to Auschwitz and shortly afterward died of heart failure, pneumonia, or circulatory collapse. Healthy young men and women between twenty and thirty suddenly succumbed to diseases that normally only killed the elderly. In light of these consequences, the blackberry leaves tasted even better.

After another hour of walking, she dragged herself up the stairs to their apartment, her toes aching in the too-small shoes from the Jewish community's second-hand shop. No sooner had she opened the door than her mother rushed over.

"Astrid, finally! Where have you been for so long?" Her Aryan mother worried every time a family member came home later than usual.

"I'm sorry, Mutti." Astrid hung her coat on the hook and slipped out of her uncomfortable shoes. "That vile SS officer threw me off the tram and I didn't have enough money for another ticket, so I had to walk."

"Oh, you poor thing. I've kept your dinner warm. Sit down at the table." Mother hurried into the tiny kitchen and returned with a plate of boiled potatoes.

"Potatoes again?" Astrid complained, although it didn't stop her from greedily stuffing the meal into her mouth. At work, she received a meal in the cafeteria, but that was many hours ago and the long walk had made her hungry.

"We don't have anything else left. I've spent the entire day running errands and couldn't even buy a turnip."

Astrid twisted her face into a grimace. Her mother, the only family member not conscripted into forced labor, took care of the majority of household chores. She spent most of the day walking from one store to another until somewhere, someone would sell her food on Jewish ration cards.

"Where are the others?"

"Your father and Hans had to leave for the night shift. Markus is asleep." Mother pushed a cup of hot herbal tea toward Astrid.

Astrid's youngest brother Markus had drawn the hardest lot: he had been assigned to a construction brigade, or rather a cleanup crew after bomb attacks, where he was forced into ten hours of back-breaking physical labor daily. Her heart contracted painfully; family was the only thing they had left. All five of them drew their strength from sticking together.

Every day, they reassured each other that the Nazi rule would eventually end, and times would get better again.

Overwhelmed by love, Astrid leaned against her mother: "I'm so glad I have you all. Our family is the single bright spot in this terrible situation."

"I feel the same way." Mother stroked her hair. "Without you children and your father, my life would be so much poorer."

Astrid often wondered what compelled her mother to stay with them. One stroke of a pen beneath the divorce papers and she could lead a normal life: She wouldn't have to live in a tiny apartment in this terrible Jewish house, tremble in fear of a house search, or be harassed at every turn.

If offered a way out of the dire situation, would Astrid stay and endure her terrible fate? Astrid closed her eyes, leaning into her mother's embrace until warmth pulsed through her limbs. No, she would never leave her family. Nothing could outweigh this feeling of belonging. In the bosom of her loved ones, she felt safe, despite the awful circumstances.

CHAPTER 6

ST. GALLENKIRCH, AUGUST 1943

The local pub was packed with men either celebrating the capture of the two Jewish women with boozy revelry or needing alcohol to suppress the horrific public execution they'd just witnessed.

Felix knew them all. Tourists were the only strangers who came to this remote area. In the evenings, they typically stayed in their guesthouses or dined in the better establishments, instead of frequenting the run-down pub.

He knew exactly who of the men present sympathized with the Nazis and who was against them. The vast majority pretended to agree with the government's policies, even if their hearts might tell a different story. Around these people, he was particularly careful and never divulged things that could get him into trouble.

Felix had no problem with concealing his true intentions; from early childhood on, his father had introduced him to the family business and drilled into him: "Silence is golden. Talking is death."

"Hello, Felix," came the voice of the young shepherd who had taken over his father-in-law's flock a few years ago.

"Hello. How's old Guido doing?"

"Don't even ask! Stubborn as a mule."

The answer made Felix smirk. Guido was well over eighty and still robust. Since handing over the sheep herd to his son-in-law, he insisted on staying up in the mountain shelter near St. Antönierjoch year-round. "Let me guess, he refuses to come down to the village during winter?"

"Yes. My wife is giving me hell about it. You know how inhospitable it can get up there. She absolutely wants her father to be safe."

"He knows the mountains even better than you and I do; nothing will happen to him," Felix tried to reassure the young shepherd.

"That won't help him if he breaks a leg. He's not a young lad anymore." The shepherd shook his head back and forth. "My wife sends me up to the shelter every two weeks to check on him. Believe me, I'd gladly spare myself the climbing; I have enough to do as it is."

Felix didn't ask what exactly the shepherd's workload consisted of. The entire family, including old Guido, was involved in resistance activities against the Nazis. So he merely grumbled: "In an emergency, there's always Balto, who can find his way to the village alone to get help."

The shepherd groaned once more. "Balto was a good sheepdog, but he's been retired for a long time; can barely walk properly anymore, let alone climb. I'm starting to think Guido won't come down to the valley because of him."

"If you'd like, I'll check on both of them when I get the chance—it's only a small detour," Felix offered.

"Thanks. I owe you one." The shepherd turned around and went to another group of men standing nearby.

Someone tapped him on the shoulder from behind. Felix

swung around and recognized his partner Karl. "Oh, it's you. I thought I might find you here."

"Schnapps? On me."

Felix waved it off.

"Come on, we need to celebrate." Karl pointed his eyes toward Fritz, the local police officer and NSDAP leader who was approaching them.

At Felix' nod, Karl grabbed three shot glasses from the tray of the waitress who was just passing by.

"Hands off!" she scolded before recognizing Karl.

"Oh, come on, we're terribly thirsty." Karl adoringly gazed at her and made a rasping sound.

She laughed. "Alright then, but just because it's you."

"Thank you, beautiful. I'll never forget this." Karl handed a shot glass to Felix and passed another one to the NSDAP leader. "Good work today, Fritz."

The bloated man with the large, red nose, result of excessive alcohol consumption, was a regular buyer of expensive Swiss spirits. "I didn't know you were in the area, Karl. Was quite surprised when I saw you on the main square earlier."

Karl kept a straight face. "I wouldn't miss such a spectacle for anything."

"Same here," growled Felix. "Even Mother walked to the village with us."

"How's Resi doing?"

"Her hip is giving her trouble, but otherwise she's still her old self."

"Give her my best regards."

Most people believed Fritz had joined the party out of conviction, but Karl and Felix, who had shared the school bench with him, knew that Fritz was solely pursuing power and money—he didn't care about ideology.

"Will do."

Fritz raised his glass. "To law and order."

"To the police," Felix toasted. He didn't want to ruin his relationship with the powerful man, because without Fritz' goodwill no business in the region prospered, neither the legal nor the illegal kind.

Fritz placed the empty glass on a table and shouted for another round, to which the waitress immediately attended.

Reluctantly, Felix accepted another shot. He had planned to find the scoundrel who had abandoned the two Jewish women up at the border. For that reason he needed to stay reasonably sober.

After pouring the schnapps down his throat, Felix asked casually, "Who led those two up to the pass?"

"You'd like to know that, wouldn't you?" Fritz examined Karl first, then Felix. "For the sake of our old friendship, I'll give you some advice: Stay away from smuggling Jews."

"We don't do that sort of thing," protested Karl.

"You should know us better. We know very well what's tolerated and what's not," Felix echoed his friend's sentiment. "We want nothing to do with Jews."

"Maybe so." Fritz rocked his head back and forth, before he peered directly into Felix' eyes. "If I ever catch you, I'll personally deliver you to the Gestapo. And then I'm going to snatch your farm and make your sister my mistress."

The notion made Felix gag.

Karl came to his rescue. "No need for threats. We're clean. Word of honor." To emphasize his words, he placed his right hand over his heart.

"Then all is well." Fritz reached for the next shot glass, this time offering none to Karl and Felix.

"In the fall, I can arrange a few bottles of top-quality brandy, if you're interested," Karl mentioned casually.

Fritz's eyes began to gleam. "Keep me posted. But I want a good price."

"You always get the best terms. You know that."

"I should hope so." Shortly after, Fritz said goodbye. "See you around."

"Phew, do you think he suspects something?" muttered Felix.

"You never know." Karl rubbed his temples. "It doesn't matter. He's much too lazy to investigate. As long as you don't get caught red-handed and we supply him with the best schnapps at a good price, nothing will happen to us."

Although Felix knew that Karl wasn't as jaded as he pretended to be, sometimes he wondered whether Karl was involved in both smuggling and forgery solely for the money.

"I'm going to ask around," he said to Karl. "The traitor poses a danger to all of us."

"Those guys over there look like they might know something." Karl pointed to a group of smugglers known for their boasting.

"I'll send Valentina over if I find out anything." Felix tapped his temple and headed toward the group sitting at a table in the corner. All but shouting, the men were trying to outdo each other with adventurous stories.

Felix could tell from their glazed eyes that they had drunk more than their share of schnapps; which was perfect for subtly questioning them. He sat down at their table and ordered a round for everyone.

"Well, Felix, how's business?" asked a stocky fellow named Bernd.

"This and that. And you? I hear there was a heap of cash as a reward for delivering the two Jewish women."

"Where'd you get that nonsense?" Bernd asked, an incredulous expression on his face.

"So it's not true? There's no bounty for Jews?" Felix rubbed his chin.

Lukas snorted. "The Nazis don't pay."

"How's the business worth it, if there's no reward?"

"Come on, you can't be that stupid. You get the money from the Jews. Then you just give Fritz a tip so he can grab them at the border."

"And Fritz plays along with the ruse?" Felix pretended to know nothing about the dirty business. Obviously he had heard rumors, but had dismissed them as shameless gossip.

"It was his idea, after all. Great way to lure the Jews out of hiding and show his superiors what a tough guy he is, while we keep the money," Heinz, a short, stocky man, chimed in.

"The trips are rigged?" Bile rose in Felix' throat. The affair was much worse than he had imagined.

Lukas cast him a suspicious look. "If you want to play, you need to buy in. Fritz gets the stake; he also says how it works."

Until now, Felix had considered his old schoolmate to be a power-hungry yet harmless fool. This conversation had taught him better. Helpless rage burned through his veins. He grabbed the full shot glass that the waitress had placed in front of him a few minutes ago and emptied it in one gulp. "Nice setup, but I'm out."

"Does little Felix have too soft a heart?" Heinz taunted him.

Bernd intervened. "The Swiss police will send them back anyway, so we might as well save them the effort. Fritz is grateful and turns a blind eye to other things in return."

"Those greedy good-for-nothings don't deserve better. If they'd been smart, they would emigrated years ago instead of dragging us into war," said Heinz.

Inwardly, Felix was boiling with rage. "Were you the one who stood them up?"

"Can you blame me?"

Felix gave no answer because he was trying hard to

restrain himself from lunging at Heinz and pummeling him with his fists. After another round of schnapps, he tapped the table. "Guys, I need the john. See you around."

As soon as he entered the men's toilet, Karl appeared. With a glance over his shoulder to ensure no one else was in the room, Karl asked: "Did you find out anything?"

"Human abysses. I'll tell you later."

"Do you know who the traitor was?"

"Heinz. That pig."

At that moment, the door swung open, and Heinz stood in the doorway. "Who's a pig?"

The anger made Felix's blood boil. Without considering the consequences, he lunged at the other man. Heinz stumbled, crashed into the opposite wall of the hallway outside the toilet, regained his balance and delivered a hook to Felix's chin.

The pain clouded his vision. He blinked several times before taking advantage of his opponent's lack of attention, punching him in the side. Tangled up in a ball, they rumbled through the hallway, crashing into walls and tables until they faced each other in the middle of the tavern, accompanied by the jeers of the other guests.

"You dirty son of a bitch!" Felix shouted above the tumult. The vein in his temple was pulsing, his only goal to avenge the death of the two refugees.

"Shut up, bastard!" Heinz shouted back. "Or I'll make mush out of you."

"Go to hell!" Felix punched and kicked at the younger, stronger man. His rage blinded him to the blows he was receiving, until two strong hands gripped his elbows in an iron hold.

"Stop it!" Fritz's mighty voice thundered through the room.

The fog of rage lifted, and Felix realized the dangerous situation he had put himself into. He groaned. "I'm sorry. It's been a tough week."

"Tough week or not. You're arrested. You can sleep off your drunkenness in the cell," Fritz decreed.

Outside in the fresh mountain air, Felix' anger subsided, and he followed Fritz like a miserable wretch. His knuckles hurt, his lip was split, and he would sport several bruises the next day. He had really gotten himself into hot water. If Heinz as much as suspected the true reason Felix had attacked him and reported it, he was done for. No one handled a friend of Jews with kid gloves. Especially not Fritz, who apparently used their misfortune for his own purposes.

On the way to the police station, suddenly Karl showed up next to him, whispering: "Say Heinz owes me a bunch of money, it might get you out of this in one piece."

Felix wasn't worried about a night in the drunk tank. He had long lost count of his stays in the local jail; it was part of the business. So far, he had always gotten off lightly—every single police officer was a customer and appreciated the occasional supply of coffee, chocolate, and other delicacies from Switzerland that Felix provided them at bargain prices.

After an uncomfortable night on the hard cot in the musty-smelling cell, he was woken by Josef, the officer on duty. Josef's cousin Christoph was one of the border guards who looked the other way for a tidy sum when Felix smuggled illegals across the border.

"Sorry for the trouble, Josef." Felix made a contrite face. "It won't be to your detriment. This afternoon I'll send Valentina to your house with a package of chocolate."

Josef's expression remained serious. He looked around nervously before whispering: "Listen to me. Heinz talks a lot. Claims you're a friend of Jews and attacked him because of the two hanged women."

Felix violently shook his head. "That's a complete lie. Heinz owes Karl and me a lot of money. He told me he's never gonna pay it, and I saw red."

"Maybe." Josef rocked his head back and forth. "I'm warning you as a friend. If Fritz finds out you're smuggling Jews across the border..." He paused for effect. "...he'll hand you over to the Gestapo—and you know what that means."

Felix swallowed the lump forming in his throat. He knew all too well what Josef alluded to; he had received enough hints in that direction. He definitely didn't want to be the next corpse swinging on the gallows for weeks.

Swallowing his fear, he replied: "Don't worry, I have nothing to hide. There's nothing I could tell the Gestapo anyway."

"Everyone says the same, but in the end, they all talk." Naked fear crept into Josef's face. "If Christoph gets caught, it'll reflect bad on me too."

Felix remained silent. Josef might be a good guy, but he could have easily been sent to make Felix talk.

"Times are getting harder. More and more people are being denounced, even by their own families. Listen to me and stay away from smuggling Jews; you can only get burned."

"Thanks for the warning. But as I said, it isn't necessary. I have nothing to do with that business." Felix buttoned up his jacket and left the station.

The march home gave him plenty of time to think. His thoughts circled endlessly. It would probably be smart to heed Josef's warning to stay away from smuggling Jews.

At that thought, resistance stirred within him. He clenched his jaw and looked toward the sky. After the perfidious things he had learned last night, he had to keep going more than ever. Otherwise, he would be driving the desperate people straight into the arms of traitors like Heinz.

The very thought weighed heavily on his soul. Although he always told Valentina it was just about the money, in reality it was his way of sticking it to the Nazis.

CHAPTER 7

GARGELLEN, AUGUST 1943

Bärbel stood in her grandmother's yard at the massive chopping block. Next to it lay an impressive stack of wood. With practiced movements, she took a piece, placed it upright on the chopping block and eyed the grain as her grandfather had taught her.

Ever since she'd been a teenager, she found it soothing to be alone with herself and nature in the fresh air. By doing hard physical labor she could disconnect, which she desperately needed in her current situation. Even weeks after her arrival in the remote mountain village, her thoughts constantly circled around her arrested fellow students. The concern for their fate was mixed with fear for her own well-being.

She had fled in blind haste without considering the consequences. If she wasn't already on the wanted list, her sudden disappearance must have surely aroused suspicion. It was only a matter of time before the Gestapo connected the dots and knocked on her grandmother's door.

By then, Bärbel had to have disappeared. Over and over, she considered options just to discard them again. Sometimes she even thought about turning herself in to avoid dragging her family into her misery.

Before she left, she wanted to make enough firewood for this winter and the next. After Grandfather's death—their four children had long left the nest and started their own families—Grandmother had done it herself. But even the seemingly indestructible woman was affected by age, and for some time now, she had needed help with the heavy work.

Bärbel was only too happy to make herself useful. She wiped the sweat from her forehead, took the heavy axe in both hands, breathing in the fresh mountain air. Forcefully, she swung back and arced the axe over her head before letting the sharp blade fall. It sank deep into the wood, making a satisfying thwack. The log split in the middle, the halves falling to the left and right of the chopping block. Bärbel bent down, picked up the pieces and threw them onto the growing pile of finished firewood.

Later in the afternoon she wanted to start stacking, another art her grandfather had taught her siblings and her. Stacking was far less strenuous than chopping, but equally meditative.

Bärbel smiled at the memory of how she and her brothers had competed to see whose stack would hold better and look more beautiful. These days, it was just about making sure it withstood the autumn storms.

She grabbed the next piece of wood, swung the axe, collected the split pieces and threw them onto the pile. A movement made her pause. Squinting her eyes, she stared into the distance. She couldn't discern anything, so she turned back to her work, until a loud voice made her jump.

"Good day!"

Bärbel turned around until she spotted a figure on a hill

behind her. She reluctantly returned the greeting and placed the next piece of wood on the chopping block.

It wasn't long before the person walked up the path to Grandmother's property and positioned herself in front of Bärbel. It was Frau Moser, who ran a guesthouse for vacationers in the village. To make matters worth, she was known for being the town gossip.

Bärbel interrupted her wood chopping. "Can I help you?"

"Aren't you Bärbel?" Frau Moser examined her curiously. "I thought you were studying medicine in Innsbruck?"

For a second, Bärbel considered telling the truth. But then the entire village would know within a day that she was hiding at her grandmother's house. Therefore, she shook her head and lied without batting an eye: "You must be confusing me with someone else. I'm Gerda."

Frau Moser pursed her lips. "I could have sworn you were Bärbel."

"I'm sorry, but you must be mistaken." An ice-cold shiver ran down Bärbel's spine as Frau Moser continued to scrutinize her. She quickly added a hopefully convincing explanation: "The Reich Labor Service sent me to help Frau Egger on the farm."

"Is that so? Trude never mentioned anything." Frau Moser didn't sound convinced.

"Frau Egger rarely goes down to the village." Bärbel couldn't resist adding a dig, "Besides, she's not a gossip."

Frau Moser furrowed her brows. "You look exactly like Bärbel. Are you by any chance related to the Eggers?"

"Not that I know of." Pure panic coursed through Bärbel's veins. She gripped the axe tighter, toying with the idea of striking Frau Moser with it, before she scolded herself for having such an absurd notion. "Excuse me, I need to get back to work. There's a lot of wood to chop."

"The resemblance is striking," Frau Moser muttered as she turned away.

Once she was out of sight, Bärbel waited a full ten minutes before walking into the house. "Grandma, where are you?"

No answer. Bärbel's breath hitched. She sensed a trap and chided herself for falling into it.

"Frau Egger, where are you?" she called louder. Yet, this call also went unanswered. She was already imagining her grandmother lying at the foot of the stairs with a broken hip.

She searched the kitchen and the pantry, ran up the stairs to the second floor, her heart beating hard against her ribs. The upper floor was empty. In her mind, images of a fall were replaced by worse ones where her grandmother was being interrogated by Gestapo agents.

I should never have come here. Guilt tightened her throat until everything went black before her eyes, and she gasped for air. As a medical student, she recognized the signs of a panic attack and sat down on the bed, forcing herself to inhale deeply and regularly. After a few minutes, the attack subsided, and she managed to think clearly again.

As she returned to the ground floor, she walked into the living room and saw a white tuft flashing through the window looking over the vegetable garden behind the house. Warmth spread through her bones. Her grandmother was sitting at the spinning wheel on the sun-drenched terrace.

"There you are, I've been looking for you everywhere."

"Do you need something?" Grandmother asked without looking up. With a soft whirring, she spun the sheep's wool into a tight thread. Fascinated, Bärbel watched as Grandmother's wrinkled hands guided the thread evenly to the spinning wheel while her foot drove the wheel at a constant rhythm.

As a teenager Bärbel had practiced spinning for an entire

summer but never managed to master it. The wool she spun usually consisted of a jumble of thick and thin spots—if the thread didn't break completely, requiring her to twist it together again.

"Frau Moser was just here."

The whirring fell silent. Grandmother looked up with an alarmed expression on her face. "What did she want?"

"To gossip, I imagine. I'm afraid she recognized me." Bärbel sat down on the wooden bench against the wall, the sun rays warming her face. Blinded by the sun she closed her eyes. "I insisted my name was Gerda and that I was doing my Reich Labor Service with you."

Grandmother let go of the thread, putting the unspun wool into a bowl. "The Moser woman has the sharpest eyes in the village and the loosest tongue to go with them."

"What should we do?" An anxious feeling constricted Bärbel's throat.

"You do nothing, Gerda." Grandmother smiled. "Right after lunch, I'll walk down to the village and find out what people are talking about."

"Isn't that too suspicious?"

"On the contrary." Grandmother stood up and walked over to sit next to Bärbel on the bench. "If I don't show up and satisfy their curiosity, the gossip squad will send someone up here tomorrow on a pretext to interrogate me and examine the striking resemblance between Gerda and my granddaughter. I'd rather be seen in the village. I need to do some shopping anyway."

"What should I do in the meantime?" Bärbel didn't like the thought of her grandmother tackling the curious innkeeper and her circle of ladies on her own.

"Nothing at all. You keep chopping wood; after all, the Reich Labor Service sent you to help me." She patted Bärbel's cheek. "Now that you're officially working for me, I'm sure I'll find several urgent tasks."

"You're impossible." Bärbel's heart warmed. One could always rely on her grandmother's resourcefulness. "What will you do if they want to verify the story?"

"Oh, my little Bärbel, Frau Moser is the village gossip, not the police."

After lunch, Bärbel asked, "Are you sure, you don't want me to accompany you?"

"So even more people may recognize you? No, you stay here." Grandmother took her coat from the hook and grabbed the large wicker basket. "While I'm away, you can invent Gerda's life story. Where is she from, anyway?"

"From Innsbruck," Bärbel answered without hesitation.

"That's a very poor choice. Half the village has relatives there. How about Graz or Krems?"

"Mother lives in Graz, so that's out of the question." Bärbel was beginning to realize that inventing a watertight life story wouldn't be trivial.

"We'll go with Krems. I won't tell the Moser woman anything else about Gerda." Grandmother kissed Bärbel on the cheek. "Everything will be fine."

"See you later. I'll work on my cover story in the meantime." As Bärbel watched her grandmother walk down the steep path to the village, she wondered how long she would be able to keep up this game of hide-and-seek.

She definitely didn't want to put her grandmother in danger.

But deep down, she already knew—sooner or later, she would.

CHAPTER 8

FRANKFURT, AUGUST 1943

Astrid rubbed her back as she climbed the creaking wooden stairs to her apartment on the second floor of the dilapidated building. She had recently been conscripted from her relatively easy job as a sorter in a tea factory to work in a munitions factory for the war effort. The endless, grueling riveting of metal parts made her ache in every bone. She was looking forward to putting her feet up and watching her mother cook, while discussing the latest speculations about the war she had picked up at the factory.

"Astrid, is that you?" Mother hurried into the hallway as soon as Astrid unlocked the apartment door, her hands fidgeting nervously on her flour-dusted apron. "A letter came for you. From the Gestapo."

Astrid froze mid-motion, the coat she had just taken off sporting the hated yellow star on the left breast hovering in the air as if it had developed a life of its own. Sweat soaked through her blouse. "What do they want?"

"You have to present yourself at the police station on

Monday." Mother held out the official letter, but Astrid made no move to take it. Instead, she held her coat in front of her like a shield.

"Does it say why I'm being summoned?" she gasped between rapid breaths. Finally remembering the coat, she hung it on the coat rack.

"Apparently, you covered the star with your arm on your way home from work."

The familiar surroundings blurred before Astrid's eyes. She had to support herself against the wall with one hand, to avoid tumbling. The bright yellow star stood out on her coat, mocking her with a sneer. Her throat tightened. She gasped for breath. In a swift movement, she turned the coat around, so the star was taunting the wall instead.

Immediately she felt better. But it was a deceptive confidence. She swallowed hard. "I'm not going."

"Of course you're going. It won't be that bad." Her mother's forced smile didn't fool Astrid, the fear in her voice was too stark.

"They can put me in a concentration camp." The words almost stuck in Astrid's throat, as panic rose in her body. Any Jew summoned to the police station was on the verge of death. Only a miracle could save her now.

"Surely not just because of the star."

"You know perfectly well that out of ten people summoned, at most one returns home." Dizziness overwhelmed her and she leaned her back against the wall for support.

"You'll definitely be that one person," Mother said with forced confidence, while her trembling hands belied her words.

Gradually, the numbness left, and Astrid regained the chutzpah that normally served her well in everyday life. The hallway was the most exposed room in the apartment, where curious neighbors lingering in the staircase might eavesdrop through the thin walls. "Let's talk in the kitchen."

As soon as her mother had closed the kitchen door behind them, Astrid burst out: "I'm not going there! Never! Every one of our acquaintances who followed such a summons was arrested. Most of them are confirmed dead by now, the others we've never heard from again."

Mother didn't answer. She picked up a knife and began peeling potatoes—so old, shriveled, and foul-smelling that only the worst hunger compelled the family to eat them. Even potatoes were currently unavailable for Jews to purchase, so the family of five survived almost exclusively on Mother's Aryan ration card together with the food Astrid's youngest brother managed to scrounge.

She looked at her mother with pleading eyes. "You can't possibly expect me to go to the police station. Once they've arrested me, it won't be long before they force me to commit suicide in my cell, or they'll deport me to a concentration camp and shoot me while 'attempting to escape'..." Her voice failed her.

"What else do you want to do, sweetheart?" Mother gently stroked Astrid's hair the way she used to do when Astrid was still a child. "If you don't go, they'll come and get you. Once they are here, they might take your brothers too. And your father." Mother's tortured expression struck Astrid deep in her soul.

She didn't want to put her family in danger, all of whom, to some extent even her mother, walked the edge of the abyss on a daily basis. "I'll run away."

"How do you plan to do that? Where will you go? You won't even make it to the nearby forest Odenwald. Unless you have Aryan papers." She examined her daughter, staying silent for a moment before adding: "We really do look very similar..."

Astrid's breath caught as she realized what her mother was insinuating.

Mother rushed to the living room, returned with her passport and held the document out to Astrid.

"That will never work." Astrid stared at the passport photo. It had been taken shortly before the war, when Mother was still bursting with energy and vitality, featuring full cheeks and bright eyes. There was no comparison to the emaciated state they both were in now.

Mother leaned over her shoulder and looked at the photograph. "The picture isn't the problem. Even I can barely recognize myself." She let her gaze wander between Astrid and the passport. "At twenty-three, you already look older than I did in this photo."

Astrid snorted. "It's the birth date. No matter how haggard and bony I am, nobody will believe I'm forty-two."

"Don't be so sure, my darling." A mischievous grin flitted across Mother's face. She stroked Astrid's sunken cheeks. "I have an idea. Come with me."

Mother pulled her into the bedroom, where in one corner stood the desk, a relic from better times before the family had been crammed into a tiny two-room apartment in a Jewish house.

Back then, Mother had worked in Father's business, who earned his living as a graphic designer. Mother's delicate ink drawings had earned much praise from customers. Now with a practiced hand she took a pen and inkwell, a small remainder of black ink sloshing inside. Carefully, she applied the tip of the pen and placed skillful strokes to transform the zero of her birth year 1901 into a 2.

"See," she said, gently blowing over the fresh writing, "now you've even aged a year."

Astrid took the passport, scrutinizing it with squinted eyes. She held the document up to the light of the bare light bulb to check the altered spot. The fresh ink was indistinguishable from the original; just a tiny shadow hinted at the former zero.

"You did that beautifully," she praised her mother.

"I didn't spend years working with ink for nothing." Mother's proud smile alone made the operation worthwhile; seeing her so satisfied had become a rarity.

"Now we just need to change your hairstyle." Mother gazed at Astrid's long, light brown curls. "If it looks exactly as in the photo, nobody will give it a second glance during an inspection."

"Oh my goodness," Astrid groaned. "You really want me walking around with a bob cut?"

"If it contributes to your safety—yes."

Astrid turned the passport in her hands. "What will you do if someone finds out?"

"I'll report the passport as stolen."

"You'll never get away with that." Astrid shook her head. "First your daughter disappears, then you can't find your passport. That's far too suspicious."

Her mother laughed out loud, and for a brief moment, she looked as young and carefree as she did in the photograph. "I'll simply tell the Gestapo you stole my passport and ran for the hills. Want to bet they'll believe me?"

"You're incorrigible." In a reversal of their roles as mother and daughter, Astrid put her hands on her hips and stared at her mother. "How is this charade supposed to end?"

"I'm doing this, because I want to embrace you unharmed after the war. That's what I'm hoping for." She hugged Astrid tight.

"Speaking of hills, where am I supposed to go anyway?" Astrid nervously ran her fingers through her curls, which would soon give way to a hideous bob cut. "As soon as you report the passport stolen, they'll fish me out at the next checkpoint."

Mother rubbed her forehead. After a while, she said: "You must leave the country."

Astrid's knees gave way beneath her. She barely managed to reach the desk chair, before she collapsed. Countless times she had dreamed of leaving Germany behind. Her family had spent years trying to emigrate. Just when they had procured the necessary papers, including an affidavit, the Nazis had issued a directive prohibiting Jews from leaving the country.

Though Mother would have been allowed to emigrate without her family, she hadn't hesitated for a second, before refusing the offer and staying with them. Astrid felt a little bit like a traitor, because she was considering abandoning her family. She pushed the thought aside.

"Where should I go? And how?"

Mother leaned against the desk, took Astrid's hands in hers, gazing intently into her eyes. "Listen to me carefully, sweetheart. There's a way for you to survive this war." She lowered her voice to a whisper. "I have a good friend in Lucerne; we've been maintaining loose contact through letters. She will help you."

"You mean Marie Steiner?"

"Exactly. I'll send her a postcard announcing your visit."

"But... the censors read everything."

Mother rubbed her forehead again. "Right. I need to think about that. I'll phrase the postcard in a way she'll understand, yet no one else will. Anyhow, you must memorize her address. If you're searched, nothing should indicate that you're planning to leave the country."

Fear constricted Astrid's throat. Perhaps it would be better to comply with the summons to the police station. Before she could express her doubts, her mother was voicing her plan. "As soon as you're in Switzerland, seek her out. She'll vouch for you, so you'll be recognized as a political refugee, and they won't send you back."

Astrid felt dizzy. "Can they actually do that? I mean, send me back?"

"There seem to have been such cases. This is the reason why you must proceed with caution. Avoid the authorities before you've consulted with Marie. And above all, don't tell anyone who you really are."

The flood of information made Astrid's head spin. "How do I get to Switzerland? I can hardly board a train in Frankfurt and simply get off in Basel."

"That's true, you really can't do that." Mother furrowed her brow. "I could try to get a travel permit, but that will take weeks."

"Besides, you'd need the passport to ask for it, which you've just forged," Astrid added.

"That's true again." Mother gave her a playful flick on the nose. "Isn't it good that I have such an intelligent daughter?"

They looked at each other in silence for a while, until Mother nodded excitedly. "Do you remember Herr Jakobi?"

"Wasn't he recently deported to Theresienstadt?"

"He was, but his two sons, Baruch and Daniel, escaped about a year ago. Herr Jakobi told me they made it across the Alps to Switzerland and from there to Palestine."

Astrid shuddered at her mother's words. It was a mixture of excited joy and panic-stricken fear. "I've never been to the Alps. How am I even supposed to find my way?"

"The two Jakobi sons didn't know their way around either. They used a guide. I'm sure I can find out the name." She turned and searched through the desk drawer until she pulled out a postcard and held it up triumphantly. "The name is Karl."

Astrid pursed her lips in a mock smile. "How many men named Karl do you think there are in the Alps?"

Mother's euphoria vanished like the air from a bursting balloon. She turned the postcard over, staring at the photo: a dark brown wooden house amidst green meadows. Flower boxes hung from every window, filled with bright red geraniums. It was the epitome of peace and tranquility.

"I remember. Herr Jakobi mentioned the name of the village: Sankt Gallenkirch in Montafon. And the guide's full name is Karl Gruber." Mother beamed from ear to ear.

Shaking her head, Astrid summarized: "Your brilliant plan is for me to travel to the Montafon valley and ask in a remote village for a man named Karl Gruber who will guide me over the mountains into Switzerland. From there, I just have to reach Lucerne, find your friend Marie Steiner, and voilà, I'll send you a postcard saying I've arrived safely."

Mother giggled. "More or less, although it won't be quite that simple."

"Even if I find this man named Karl, he won't smuggle me across the border out of the goodness of his heart. I suspect he'll expect payment for his services." The anticipation faded. In its stead despair spread through Astrid's limbs. She leaned her cheek against Mother's stomach. "We don't have the money."

"This isn't a reason to give up." A grim expression on her face, Mother pulled her golden wedding band from her finger and placed it on Astrid's finger. "Take this. It's the most valuable thing I own. You can trade or sell it to pay the guide."

Astrid looked at the shimmering ring. Her mother's generous gesture warmed her heart. "Are you sure you want to give up your wedding band?"

"Absolutely." Mother's eyes glistened with moisture. "I would do much more for you, my sweetheart."

Astrid sat motionless on the chair, thoughts whirling in her head. "What will Father say when he finds out?"

"You can ask him yourself as soon as he comes home. But I know he'll agree. He loves you just as much as I do and would do anything to keep you safe."

For several minutes Astrid sat motionless, her gaze fixed on the golden ring on her finger. Eventually, she murmured: "I don't want to leave you."

"Then you'll have to try your luck at the police office on Monday." Mother gave her a stern look. "Believe me, I'd rather keep you with me, too."

Astrid had to swallow hard. The longer she thought about it, the greater became her concerns. Then she remembered the many acquaintances and friends who had received similar summons and had never returned to their families.

Everything inside her ached at the threat. She was far too young to die. At twenty-three, she had her entire life ahead of her, although it seemed not in Germany and not with her family, as long as Hitler remained in power and mercilessly persecuted the Jews.

She straightened her shoulders. "I'll do it. And I promise I'll write you a postcard as soon as I'm with your friend in Lucerne, so you'll know I'm fine and won't have to worry anymore."

Mother stroked her hair. "We should agree on a code."

"How about: The sun shines over the mountains and we go for lots of walks. Lake Lucerne invites swimming."

"It'll be a bit too cold by the time you get there." A wistful expression appeared on Mother's face. "Better write: We're feeding the ducks at Lake Lucerne."

"Great idea." Astrid stood up and embraced her mother. For several minutes they clung to each other until Mother broke away.

"You'll succeed, I'm sure. Let's prepare for your journey; there's still much to organize, starting with your new hairstyle." Mother pulled scissors from the desk drawer, clicking them together.

Disgusted, Astrid looked at the instrument in Mother's hand. Losing her long, curly hair would be painful. "Do we really need to do this?"

"We can't take any unnecessary risks. You want to resemble your passport photo, don't you?"

Astrid nodded.

"Sit down. As long as it's just your hair that you have to sacrifice, you should consider yourself lucky."

Reluctantly, Astrid obeyed. With each strand that fell to the floor, the finality of the farewell settled deeper into her soul. She didn't want to lose her family. But even more, she wanted to survive.

Her beautiful long hair was a small price to pay for the hope of a better life.

CHAPTER 9

SEPTEMBER 1943, SANKT GALLENKIRCH

Felix sat at the kitchen table with his sister Valentina and Karl. The petroleum lamp cast flickering shadows on the wall.

"I have two people who want to escape. They are from Vienna and pay well."

"No." Valentina's voice was sharp. "We've talked about this. No more Jews."

"Val—" Felix began, but she cut him off.

"Have you forgotten what happened to the two women? Do you want to end up on the gallows, too?"

"Nothing will happen. Everything's gone according to plan so far," Karl reassured her as he twirled his empty schnapps glass between his fingers.

"That's easy for you to say. You're not risking your neck on the trip." Valentina glared at him, her eyes flashing furiously.

"Neither are you. Let Felix decide for himself." Karl glared back just as grimly.

Before the two could start a fight, Felix intervened. "Would you like another schnapps, Karl?"

"No, thanks. Otherwise I won't be able to walk down to the village."

Despite her anger, Valentina offered, "You can stay overnight. The twins are on flak duty in Innsbruck."

"That's kind of you, but I need to leave for Bregenz at the crack of dawn tomorrow." Karl stood up. "Think about it, Felix. The couple will pay good money."

"Smuggling coffee and chocolate pays well too," Valentina snapped.

Karl ignored her objection. He slipped on his jacket, put on his hat and tipped the brim. "I'll return within a week, make up your mind in the meantime."

After Karl left, Valentina turned to her brother. "You promised, Felix. After the last tour, you swore you would stop guiding Jews across the border."

"I promised to take a break." Felix had no desire to have this discussion. But Valentina wouldn't let up until the matter was settled. He poured himself a large glass of water and drank it in one go, while his sister watched him with a grim expression.

"My last trip was over two months ago. Don't you think enough time has passed?"

She stared at him in disbelief. "You can't possibly be serious. Have you already forgotten Josef's warning?"

"No, I haven't..." Felix massaged his neck.

"Why are you insisting on risking your life? We earn enough with the usual goods. For which, by the way, you'd spend at most one night in jail if they catch you."

Felix leaned back and stared at the wooden ceiling, where the shadows of the flickering petroleum lamp performed a bizarre dance. The situation had been gnawing at him for months. He could no longer in good conscience stand on the sidelines watching people being slaughtered in cold blood. "It's not about the money, Vale."

"Then what is it about?" She pursed her lips.

"You read the newspaper and listen to the radio, don't you? What's happening to the Jews..." He ran his hands through his hair. "I can't stand by any longer while these people are sent to their deaths."

"On the contrary, that is exactly the reason why you shouldn't be taking Jews to the border. If they're caught up in the mountains, they'll be executed."

"That's the crux. If I don't do it, someone else will. Heinz for example, who will one hundred percent betray the couple to the Gestapo. He'll pocket the Jews' money for the passage and deliver them straight to the gallows." Anger burned through Felix's limbs as he thought about the rigged game Fritz and some of the guides were playing.

Valentina put her hands on her hips. "It's not your job to avenge the misdeeds of other people."

"Is it really not?" Felix poured himself a schnapps, turning the glass between his fingers. "Tell me you can watch with a clear conscience how these people put their trust in Heinz."

"That's not what this is about." Valentina squirmed uncomfortably in her chair.

"On the contrary, that's exactly what it's about. If I refuse this job, I become complicit."

"You're crazy." She tapped her forehead. "You can't save the entire world."

"Not the entire world, but at least a few Jews." Felix downed the brandy. It burned down his throat, warming him from within. "I'm having nightmares."

"You? Why this?"

He shook his head as if he could dispel the dark thoughts. "Every night when I close my eyes, I see the two women hanging from the gallows. In my dreams, they're alive and talking to me. They look at me with mortal fear. They lament the terrible things that were done to them. And there's always the silent reproach that I did nothing to stop it."

"You know that ghosts don't exist, right?" Despite her assertions, Valentina had turned chalk-white. "It's pure imagination. The Jewish women aren't really speaking to you."

"I know." Felix groaned, tapping his forehead. "It's just in here. But that doesn't change anything. I don't want to blame myself for looking the other way and doing nothing."

"What about me? And my fear for you?" Valentina's voice trembled. "Every time you're out there, I lie awake at night. I dread the day they are going to catch you."

"You shouldn't think that way." Helplessly, Felix looked at his sister, who had been his best friend, his confidante, his business partner and occasionally his surrogate mother for decades.

"Do you think I don't see what the Nazis are doing to the Jews? I don't agree with it either." She poured herself a shot, drank it in one gulp and set it down on the wooden table with a loud bang. "Of course I feel sorry for them. But first and foremost I have to think about my family. I have five children to provide for and our mother. What will become of us if they send you to a camp?"

Felix buried his face in his hands. Valentina had hit his sore spot. Since her husband had died, he'd been the family's breadwinner. What little the farm produced wasn't enough to feed them. It weighed heavily on his conscience that he might be letting the family down.

With forced bravado, he said, "You'll manage without me. You're the better mountaineer anyway and you know the business inside out. It wouldn't be a problem for you to do the tours yourself."

Valentina shook her head. "Keep lying to yourself. If Fritz

accuses you of treason, he'll take us all into custody. He's had his eye on the farm for a long time."

An icy shiver ran down Felix's back as he remembered Fritz's words: *If I ever catch you, I'll personally deliver you to the Gestapo. And then I'll take your farm and make your sister my mistress.* He hoped Valentina didn't suspect anything of the fate intended specifically for her.

The light of the petroleum lamp danced across her face, making the lines around her mouth appear deeper. It broke his heart to see his sister so depressed, but he couldn't let it influence him. "I have to do this. If everyone looks away, there's no hope for a better future"

"You and your damned ideals." Her gentle voice belied the harsh words. "You've always been a hopeless romantic."

"So, you agree with my plan?" Hope sprouted within him. He didn't want to fall out with Valentina, but ultimately he would smuggle the Jews without her approval.

"Can I change your mind?" She laughed bitterly.

He shook his head.

"Do you remember what Father always said?" She looked at the portrait on the wall showing their father, wearing a traditional hat with a bird feather and the inevitable pipe in the corner of his mouth. "'Stay out of politics.' He was right."

"Father has been dead for more than two decades. Back then the Nazis didn't exist," Felix replied. "This stopped being about politics a long time ago. It's about decency. And human lives."

"Do what you must do." Valentina shrugged.

"I want you to be fine with my actions. I need your support. Please."

"Alright. But only if you're more careful than ever. At the slightest sign something is wrong, you abort. And you do a maximum of one trip including Jews per month."

Felix leaned back in relief. "I promise. Thank you for having my back."

"Someone has to look out for you. I'll send you a warning, if something goes wrong."

"All right." Years ago, they had agreed that Valentina would light the chimney next to the house if he should stay away from the farm. So far, they had used the warning signal once: when her husband had been drafted into the Wehrmacht and there was a chance they would come for Felix too. "But how can I answer you?"

She furrowed her brow. Several seconds later she said, "I have an idea! You take a hand mirror with you and direct the sunlight to the kitchen window."

"A fantastic idea!" Secretly, Felix was relieved that he'd been able to persuade her so quickly. "I'll use it to flash my initials in Morse code, so you know I've seen the smoke."

"And I'll reply with the number of the emergency hiding place where we'll meet." For many years, they had used well-hidden depots to temporarily store smuggled goods before distributing them to buyers.

"That's a plan." She stood up, put the glasses in the sink and then turned to him. "I'm going to bed, there's a lot of work to do in the morning."

Felix listened to her footsteps walking upstairs to her room, which she shared with her youngest daughter. He, however, stayed in the kitchen for a long time, thinking. He hoped that he wouldn't regret his decision to help the Jews.

CHAPTER 10

Astrid had left Frankfurt in pouring rain, equipped with a backpack and some cash her family had scraped together from friends and acquaintances. Her mother's gold wedding ring graced her finger. When she arrived in Sankt Gallenkirch after several days of exhausting travel, the rain had finally subsided to a fine drizzle.

She had deliberately used slow local trains that were crowded by commuters, women with small children, merchants selling goods, and whoever else needed to travel from one place to another. Fortunately, her mother's passport had withstood every—admittedly cursory—inspection.

Gray clouds hung low in the mountains, swallowing the peaks and plunging the village into an eerie twilight. After days of continuous rain the streets were muddy, water collecting in deep puddles.

Occasionally, people darted through the village, their heads buried deep in upturned coat collars. No one greeted, no one stopped, which was to Astrid's advantage. She wanted as little contact with the villagers as possible, since she didn't want to answer curious questions, and even less did she want anyone to remember her.

At the inn called Traube, whose metal sign featured a painted green vine next to a wine glass, she summoned all her courage and asked for a room for the night.

The innkeeper was a buxom woman with gray streaks in her dark hair, who looked as if she had worked hard all her life. "I'm sorry, we only rent to guests in summer. Try the Zur Post inn at the main square."

"Thank you." Astrid left and walked in the direction of the main square. From a distance, she spotted the Zur Post inn, when its door opened and two men in SS uniforms stepped out. Her heart hammering viciously, Astrid turned a corner. She walked on aimlessly while considering how risky it would be to stay at an inn that apparently was frequented by SS men.

After a few minutes, she decided it was best to look for another place and return to Zur Post just in case she couldn't find anything else. Meanwhile the drizzle had completely soaked through, and her socks squeaked in her wet shoes with every step. Shivering, she paced through narrow alleys until she spotted a two-story house at the edge of the village with blooming geraniums in front of the windows and a sign: "Room available."

This was perfect: away from the village center and, from the looks of it, right on the road that led up into the mountains.

When she rang the bell, a plump woman with a friendly face answered the door. "What can I do for you?"

"I'm looking for a room."

"You're lucky, I have one available. Come in." The woman turned the sign on the door, so it now read: "Room occupied."

"How long would you like to stay?"

"A few days. I've only been granted a week of vacation." During the long journey, Astrid had worked out a viable cover story.

"Come with me, and I'll show you the room. We'll handle the formalities if you like it."

Astrid followed the innkeeper, eyeing the inn with curiosity. The old wooden staircase to the first floor creaked with every step. In the hallway hung pictures of mountain landscapes and a painted cupboard stood against the wall.

The innkeeper stopped in front of a door, took out a huge bundle of keys from the pocket in her apron and opened the door. "This is the room."

Astrid entered the small, cozy place. A single bed covered by red-and-white checkered bedding stood against the wall, next to it a small nightstand with an oil lamp. On the short side were two shelves nailed to the wall as well as some clothes hooks beside the door. Despite the pretty sight, Astrid shivered.

The innkeeper must have noticed. "We don't heat the bedroom. But you're welcome to go downstairs to the guest room at any time. At night, you'll be nice and warm under the thick down comforter and if that doesn't suffice, I'll make you a hot water bottle to take upstairs."

"That's very kind of you. Thank you. I'll take the room."

"It's an unusual time of year to come to us in the Montafon. Most guests visit during the summer or in winter to go skiing. What brings you to the area?"

Astrid peered into the sympathetic face of the woman, whom she instinctively trusted. Regardless, she exercised caution. "The desire for undisturbed sleep. I live in the Ruhr area and wish for nothing more than to sleep through a few nights in an actual bed. It's truly no pleasure to rush down to the cellar during air raid alarms almost every night."

"Oh, you poor thing." The innkeeper gave her the once

over. "You need some feeding up, too. Isn't there anything to eat in the city?"

"Not as plentiful as before." Astrid was treading on thin ice. Criticizing the regime—even on such harmless matters as lacking food supplies—could be taken the wrong way, especially since city dwellers, though suffering from shortages, still had enough not to go hungry—unlike Jews.

"Well, I'll be sure to put plenty of bacon in the stew." The innkeeper beamed at her. "Dinner is at half past six."

Astrid followed the woman downstairs to the reception, where she signed into the guest book. Just as she was about to leave, a burly man appeared. He was carrying a beer keg in his muscle-packed arms and asked the innkeeper in passing, "Do you know when Karl is coming by again? Our stock is running low."

"I'll make a note of it." The innkeeper explained to Astrid, "That was my husband, by the way. He's responsible for inventory."

Astrid was about to leave when she reconsidered and asked, "Excuse me, were you just talking about Karl Gruber?"

"Yes, do you know him?"

Inwardly, Astrid rejoiced. Finding the smuggler had been easier than she'd expected. Yet she didn't intend to reveal her true intentions. "Not personally, but I've heard quite a bit about him. My mother's birthday is coming up and I'd like to get her something special. It is said Karl can procure absolutely anything."

"People say a lot of things." The innkeeper shrugged her shoulders.

"If you tell me where I can find him, I'll ask him myself."

"That won't help you. He's been gone for a few days, and nobody knows when he'll return." The woman squinted her eyes. "If it's urgent, ask Heinz. You'll find him most nights in the pub at the end of the street." She pointed in the direction with her hand.

"Thank you very much, I'll do that."

The innkeeper checked if the guest book was filled out correctly, before she closed it. "Is your husband at the front, Frau Hambach?"

"I'm not..." Astrid caught herself just in time. Since she was traveling with her mother's passport, she had to pretend to be married. Of course, she couldn't mention that her father, or rather husband, was Jewish. "I mean, he..." she cleared her throat. "He's been missing in action."

"I'm sorry to hear that. You mustn't give up hope."

Astrid tried to put on a sad expression. "I won't. Every day I pray to receive news from him. Thank you again for everything. I'll see you at dinner."

In her room, Astrid considered whether she should hop over to the pub right away. Then she shook her head. Heinz probably wouldn't be there until after dinner anyway.

Instead, she put her belongings on the shelves. When she was done, she changed her mind and packed everything into her backpack in case she needed to leave in a hurry. She sat down on the bed, and gazed at the cloud-shrouded mountains, twisting her mother's wedding ring, which sat loosely on her finger. So far, the cash had sufficed, although very little was left after paying for the accommodation.

She hated the thought of having to trade the ring, since it was the link to her family. Apart from an old family photo taken on the occasion of her youngest brother's birth almost two decades prior, she hadn't brought anything that might indicate her heritage.

Long before it was time for dinner, she combed her hair, smoothed her skirt, and walked downstairs to the guest room because she wanted to have a look around—and because it was miserably cold in her room.

A gaunt man with a balding head and horn-rimmed glasses, seemingly absorbed in a book, sat next to the tiled stove. When Astrid entered the cozy warm room, he raised his head, looking at her with relief. "It's about time. What took you so long, Martha?"

Sensing a trap, Astrid froze mid-movement. Her throat constricting, barely letting her croak, "Excuse me, you must be confusing me with someone else."

Suspicion flitted through his eyes as they inspected her. "Didn't Karl send you?"

A storm of emotions tumbled through her insides. Somehow Astrid clung to her composure. "You mean the smuggler? You know him?"

"So he did send you?" He stood up and approached Astrid. Upon closer inspection, she noticed his sunken cheeks, the dark circles beneath his eyes behind the horn-rimmed glasses and his hunted look. Intuitively, she sensed that he was on the run, too. Her heart pounded at the realization that he might be a Jew, trying to escape to Switzerland.

After making sure there were no unwanted listeners in the room, she positioned herself so she had the door in her view. "No, Karl didn't send me. However, I am looking for him."

He didn't flinch. "Can it be a coincidence that you appear right now in this room?"

"It's only a coincidence that we're here at the same time." She spotted a loose thread on the left breast of his shabby sweater and sighed with relief. A Gestapo informant wouldn't go as far as to put remnants of the Jewish star on his clothing. "After all, we want to use the same service."

"And what would that be?" He was on his guard.

"Safe passage over the mountains." She pointed to the place where the star had been. "To escape persecution."

The man turned pale. "I..."

"There's no need to worry. I'm Jewish too, half-Jewish to be precise, which is the reason I'm looking for Karl."

Relief spread across his features. He gave a slight bow. "Allow me to introduce myself. Bruno Weinberg, former antiques dealer from Vienna."

As a precaution, she used her mother's name, under which she had registered with the innkeeper. "The pleasure is all mine. Sieglinde Hambach, housewife from Frankfurt."

"A beautiful name, if a bit old-fashioned for a young woman."

Dismayed, she swallowed the budding panic. "My mother has a fondness for the Nibelungen saga. When she had a girl, she named me Sieglinde."

Herr Weinberg motioned for her to sit with him at the table next to the tiled stove. In a low voice, he explained, "This morning, my... well, my pretend wife was supposed to arrive here. But she hasn't shown up." A shadow flitted across his face, as if he feared for the worst. "Who knows what happened. Maybe she was just delayed."

"I'm sure she'll arrive soon. Transportation is very unreliable these days," Astrid reassured him.

"Karl arranged the papers. I don't know Martha, but he said a married couple would be less suspicious than two single people traveling." He buried his head in his hands. "Do you actually believe something came up? Isn't it much more likely that she was arrested?"

In that moment, the door opened, and the innkeeper stepped inside, holding two steaming bowls of goulash soup. After setting the table she left the room, explaining to her guests that she had to feed the pigs.

Astrid spooned the hearty goulash soup in silence, struggling with herself until she finally set the spoon aside. Locking eyes with Herr Weinberg, she said, "Take me with you. Please."

He rubbed his chin. With an earnest expression, his eyes seemed to bore deep into her soul, wanting to read whether her request was genuine. After a while, his features relaxed. "I see no reason why you shouldn't tag along. However, it's not my decision, but that of our guide Felix. We're supposed to meet him tomorrow morning."

"Felix?" Astrid immediately sensed a trap. Alarmed, she asked, "Didn't you say Karl arranged the escape?"

Herr Weinberg smiled. "One can tell you're truly persecuted."

"This was a test?" Her nervousness disappeared. She was even a little proud to have passed her counterpart's trial.

"No. At least I didn't intend it. The guide's name is indeed Felix. Karl is the contact, who arranged everything." He tilted his head and studied her once more. "One can't be prudent enough. A few months ago, two women in our situation were betrayed and hanged. There are rumors that some guides work for the Gestapo."

Violent goosebumps broke out all over Astrid's body. The danger was worse than she had suspected.

"Therefore I made inquiries beforehand. Both Karl and Felix have an unblemished reputation. So far, everyone who has entrusted their life to them has arrived safely in Switzerland."

"That's a great relief." Astrid slowly exhaled until the scrawling spiders on her skin disappeared. "If you allow, I'll accompany you to the meeting point tomorrow morning and ask the guide if he'll take me along."

"I would be delighted. Even if Martha still arrives in time, a third person won't hurt."

"A thousand thanks. I'm deeply in your debt."

"Don't thank me before we've crossed the border."

During the remainder of dinner, they chatted about this and that. Actually Herr Weinberg did most of the talking, entertaining her with all sorts of funny anecdotes from his time as a wealthy Viennese antiques dealer.

It was a refreshing change from the monotony of the past days. Since leaving her home, she had constantly been on her guard, exchanging nothing more than a few polite phrases with other people.

When Herr Weinberg said goodnight, Astrid too retired to her room, where she snuggled under the cozy down comforter. Just before falling asleep, a smuggler called Heinz flashed through her mind. Immediately she bolted upright in her bed. Despite the cold, beads of sweat trickled from her forehead as she wondered if this man, to whom she had planned to entrust herself, was one of the Gestapo informants Herr Weinberg had warned her about.

She shook her head. If Felix refused to take her along, she would have to be extra careful.

CHAPTER 11

A few weeks after the encounter with Frau Moser, Bärbel stood at the kitchen sink scrubbing pots. Through the window she spotted her grandmother trudging up from the village, bent under the heavy load of shopping bags.

She had repeatedly offered to take over running the errands, but Grandmother had waved her off. "If you rest, you rust. I'm not too old to make the trip down to the village. Besides, you don't want to be recognized. Have you forgotten that detail already?"

Bärbel had agreed reluctantly. At least she could rush outside to meet her grandmother at the edge of the property. She untied her apron and hurried outside. "Did you get everything we need?"

"We need to talk." Bärbel flinched at the ominous words.

"What happened, Grandma?"

"Nothing yet." Grandmother handed Bärbel the shopping bags and followed her into the house. While her grandma removed her headscarf and coat, Bärbel unpacked the bags in the kitchen.

"Leave it be. We'll do that later," said the old woman, who was usually meticulous about cleanliness and order.

The hair on Bärbel's neck stood on end. Fear pooling deep in her stomach, she slowly turned around. "Bad news?"

"Sit down, my child." Grandmother's voice sounded downright eerie. "After your encounter with Frau Moser, she made inquiries with the Reich Labor Service. As expected, they know nothing about sending some Gerda to help me."

Bärbel felt the blood drain from her face. Grateful she was sitting on the kitchen bench, she leaned against the backrest. The words all but stuck in her throat as she asked, "What shall I do?"

Her grandmother sidled up to her and patted her hand. "Wait. For now, Frau Moser's curiosity is satisfied. Perhaps she won't take further action."

Bärbel shook her head vigorously. "I doubt that! You know Frau Moser. Remember the missing apple pie when I was ten? She turned half the village upside down because she was convinced I'd stolen it from her windowsill. She stood with new evidence at your door every day for three weeks straight, until someone found out her own cat had nibbled the pie."

Grandmother fiddled with her hair bun. "People can change."

"Not Frau Moser. Otherwise she wouldn't have bothered making inquiries with the Reich Labor Service in the first place." The queasiness from her stomach crept up her throat.

Meanwhile her grandmother's wrinkled face had turned chalk-white beneath her summer tan. "You must leave until I've convinced Frau Moser and the rest of the village that you've returned to Innsbruck."

"I can't go back, or I'll be arrested immediately." Bärbel swallowed the rising desperation.

"That's not what I meant. You need to hide somewhere for

the time being. Once things have blown over, you can return." Grandmother seemed to believe that Frau Moser and the police would eventually give up the search.

Bärbel had a different opinion, but she clung to any glimmer of hope. "Where should I hide?"

"Hmm." Grandmother sighed. "I don't have a good idea. The barn, the shed, the attic... all too risky. If they come looking for you, they'll turn the farm upside down."

"I could stay with Mother."

Grandmother shook her head. "That's too obvious. You need to hide someplace, where no one will expect you."

Bärbel frantically searched for a solution until she remembered the cave halfway up the ridge where she and her brothers had often played in their childhood. They had named it the Smuggler's Cave and Grandfather had helped them to make the space comfortable. He had built a bench from boards and allowed them to line the floor with old horse blankets. Once, the children had even spent the night in the cave, admittedly during summer when temperatures reached nearly ninety degrees.

"I'll hide in the mountains."

Grandmother grabbed her hand. "Do you think that's a good idea? It's early October, soon it'll get quite cold up there."

"Do you remember how we as children used to go to the—"

"Stop!" Grandmother interrupted. "I don't want to know anything. Then I can't reveal anything if I'm interrogated."

Images of her beloved grandmother in the hands of the Gestapo attacked Bärbel, causing her to swallow down the bile in her throat. Ignorance wouldn't help her grandmother, since the Gestapo wouldn't believe she knew nothing. Nonetheless, it was admirable that the old woman was willing to take this risk to protect her granddaughter.

Dusk was settling over the valley when Bärbel said, "I'll leave at the crack of dawn tomorrow."

"Until then, we have time to work out a plan. Now, let's put away the groceries and have some hot cocoa."

Bärbel nestled against her grandmother, grateful that she could always rely on her. "Thank you, Grandma. I'm sorry for putting you in danger."

"Nonsense." The old woman lovingly tousled her hair. "That's what grandmothers are for, after all."

While they drank the cocoa, they planned the details of Bärbel's hiding. "When the coast is clear and you can return, I'll hang the yellow bedsheet out the window in the upstairs chamber every morning."

"Every couple of days I'll go to the lookout point from where I can see the sheet. Is there anything else I need to consider?"

"I can't think of anything right now. Go pack your things so you won't waste time in the morning."

With a heavy heart, Bärbel climbed the narrow wooden stairs. She surveyed the small room where she had spent happy vacations surrounded by her family. Memories of her carefree childhood years flooded her brain: she and her brothers romping outdoors from dawn till dusk. Back then, her biggest concern had been who would get the largest piece of homemade apple pie. Today, she was the only one of the three siblings alive—and perhaps not for much longer.

Her belongings fit into her grandfather's old leather backpack: two sets of underwear, a warm sweater, her thickest socks, and a summer dress. Plus some money and the silver bracelet she had received for her First Communion. How long ago since she had been an excited ten-year-old in a beautiful white dress and brand-new shiny shoes she'd got for the occasion. A wistful smile appeared on her face as she sat on the bed, staring out of the window into the night. The snow-covered mountain peaks reflected the bright moonlight.

From a distance, she thought she heard wolf howls. Although she knew wolves were practically extinct in the area, and that a solitary animal wouldn't attack a human, goosebumps spread across her arms.

Perhaps she should take along Grandfather's old hunting rifle? Then she shook her head. It wasn't wild animals she needed to fear, but humans. After giving it a second thought, she dismissed the idea. In an emergency, she wouldn't be capable of shooting a person, and carrying a gun would make her look suspicious.

Her gaze wandered across the familiar little room until it stopped at the school desk that her father and one of her uncles had sanded, polished, painted bright green, and carried upstairs so that Bärbel and her brothers would have a place to draw on rainy days.

Suddenly, it seemed as if Mother was standing next to her in the room, looking over her shoulder. "Don't you want to join us in the living room, Bärbel?"

"No, Mutti. I want to finish this drawing first." Beaming with pride Bärbel showed her the sheet of paper on which she had meticulously drawn the human spine. "Look, here are the vertebrae. And there's the spinal cord. I need to know all this if I'm going to be a doctor someday."

A deep sigh escaped from her chest. By fleeing Innsbruck, she had abandoned her medical studies. Her chances of being re-admitted to university diminished with each day she stayed away unexcused. She took a deep breath, gathering up her courage. "After the war, different rules will apply. Once the Nazis are gone you can continue your studies."

She wished she could write a letter to her mother explaining why she had disappeared without a word of goodbye. Unfortunately that was impossible. Since letters were censored, she could make vague hints at best. By now, her mother had probably figured out Bärbel's whereabouts after Grandmother had called her from the village, giving encrypted information.

As she entered the kitchen with her packed backpack, a considerable supply of foodstuffs was waiting for her. On the table lay apples and pears from the cellar, a large piece of smoked bacon, cheese, a package of zwieback, a small bag of dried peas, an emergency can of corned beef that had been slumbering in the pantry for years, and a small pouch of salt. Next to the food lay a flashlight, candles, and matches.

"This should last you a good week. If the coast isn't clear by then, I'll leave a package for you up by the ruins under the big pine tree."

Bärbel hugged her tightly. "Grandma, you're the best!"

"I wish I could do more for you, my sweetheart."

They sat together for a while and talked, deliberately avoiding the topic of the impending escape. Eventually, Grandmother looked at the clock. "You should go and get some sleep; you have a strenuous day ahead of you."

The next morning, Bärbel woke up before the rooster crowed. She took one last gaze around the small room before descending the creaking stairs to the kitchen. There, Grandmother was waiting for her with a hearty breakfast.

"I'm not hungry."

"Eat something anyway; you can't march well on an empty stomach."

Despite her nostalgic mood, Bärbel had to smile. Although she had believed she couldn't swallow a bite due to her nerves, she emptied the plate of fried eggs, bacon, and baked beans, and afterward dug into a thick slice of buttered bread. Who knew when she would have such a princely meal again? Cooking in the cave probably wasn't an option.

Just as she shouldered the heavy backpack, a shrill

sputtering cut through the silence. Her heart beating wildly, she peered through the kitchen window. A motorcycle turned into the yard and a man in uniform dismounted.

"Good heavens, that must be Josef." Grandmother had immediately recognized the policeman from Sankt Gallenkirch. "Quick, leave through the back door. Wait there until I've lured him into the kitchen, so he won't be able to see you."

"Thanks again for everything." Bärbel hugged her grandmother one last time before slipping into the living room. There, she passed through the terrace door, pulling it firmly shut from the outside. She crept around the corner and crouched against the wall to listen. Heavy footsteps approached the door. When thunderous knocking sounded, she gave a start.

Shortly after, the front door was opened and her grandmother said, "Josef, what are you doing here at this ungodly hour? I hope it's not bad news." Grandmother gasped, and Bärbel imagined her dramatically clutching her heart. "Has something happened to one of my sons?"

"No, Trude, I'm here for another reason. May I come in?"

"Of course."

As the door closed, Bärbel crept back toward the corner of the house. She wanted to make sure the coast was clear and risked a glance into the living room just as the door opened and Josef, followed by her grandmother, entered.

Bärbel quickly dropped to the ground, hoping he hadn't noticed her. She had known him since her childhood as a lawful, not overly strict man. But even if he wasn't a staunch Nazi, she couldn't expect leniency, because his sense of duty was too strong.

Silently crouching against the wall, she listened to the conversation drifting through a tilted window.

"Is Bärbel with you?" His question sounded more like a statement than a question.

"No," Grandmother answered, surprisingly composed.

"Come on, Trude. We've known each other for over forty years. The alleged Gerda from the Reich Labor Service, is in reality Bärbel, isn't she?"

The silence stretched on. Bärbel hardly dared to breathe. Finally, Grandmother sighed and admitted, "Yes, it's her." Bärbel's heart skipped a beat. "But she left last night."

The policeman snorted in disbelief. "Don't tell me fairy tales, Trude. She just happened to leave? What was she doing here anyway? Isn't she studying medicine in Innsbruck?"

To Bärbel's astonishment, her grandmother improvised a story on the spot, as adeptly as she spun yarn from sheep's wool. "It's such a sad story, Josef. You must remember that she always wanted to be a doctor, don't you?"

Josef grunted his agreement.

"Well, it seems she couldn't handle the demands of the university and dropped out of her studies. The poor thing didn't dare tell her parents. Therefore she came to me. You know my son, how strict he can be…"

"I've always said women have no business going to university," grumbled the policeman.

"These are modern times, Josef. Young girls don't just want to be housewives anymore." Bärbel could imagine her grandmother's bittersweet expression. Had she been born half a century later, she would have pursued a profession too.

"Why did she lie to Frau Moser?"

Grandmother groaned dramatically. "For a solid week, I tried to convince the frightened child that her parents would find out eventually and that it would be better for them to hear it from her than to read it in an official letter from the university. She was just beginning to understand when Frau Moser showed up. Our little Bärbel panicked. You should have seen how she begged me not to tell anyone the truth. The thought of her parents learning about her dropping out from Frau Moser was simply too much. You know how tactless that woman can be."

Bärbel bit her tongue to keep from laughing out loud. Frau Moser thrived on intrigue; if there was an opportunity to cause discord somewhere, she was always first in line.

"Where is Bärbel now?"

"Probably in Innsbruck. She hurried yesterday evening to catch the last train. Let's discuss it in the kitchen, shall we? I was just having breakfast and can make you some warm milk with honey."

"Who can say no to such an offer? I've always liked your honey, even as a child, Trude."

Bärbel listened until the footsteps moved away from the living room and the kitchen door closed with a loud bang. This was her cue. Carefully, she got up and crept hunched over across the terrace to the vegetable garden. Her heart pounded in her throat as she hurried between the autumnal plants toward the chicken coop and from there to the nearby forest edge.

Once she reached the protective trees, she risked a look back. The motorcycle still stood in the yard; everything was quiet. The policeman had bought Grandmother's story. Bärbel climbed the steep path into the mountains at a rapid pace. The heavy backpack cut deep into her shoulders, but she didn't dare take a break. Fear drove her relentlessly forward. Only occasionally did she stop a few seconds to wipe the sweat from her forehead and look over her shoulder. Far and wide no pursuers could be seen or heard.

The higher she climbed, the more she doubted her reckless plan. The Smuggler's Cave lay off the path. To reach it, one had to cross a flat meadow where no trail marked the way.

Would she even be able to find the place again after so many years had passed?

After a good hour of brisk climbing, the distinctive rock formation, which she and her siblings had used for orientation as children, appeared in her sight. "Past the Eagle Rock on the left, across the meadow toward the three tall pine trees," she rehearsed her oldest brother's directions.

It felt as if it was yesterday that they had played smugglers and customs officers up here, hiding and chasing each other. Confidence flowed through her limbs. Suddenly she knew exactly where the cave entrance was. After another ten minutes, she stood directly in front of the opening, half hidden by blackberry bushes. Nothing had changed. Taking a deep breath, she carefully pushed the vines aside and slipped into the cave. Inside, the smell of earth wafted into her nose, along with something else. Sniffing she felt her way deeper inside until she recognized the faint smell as cold cigarette smoke.

Someone must have been here. There were just a handful of people who knew about the cave. She and her brothers, of course—and Grandfather. The three of them had since died. The boys were the two oldest grandchildren of old Wallner from Sankt Gallenkirch. Old Wallner had fallen to his death in a mountain accident a year prior to Bärbel and her brothers finding the cave, and his son Felix had taken over the family business.

She wrinkled her nose, trying to remember what had become of his nephews. Then she shrugged. According to her grandmother, Felix continued to smuggle goods from Switzerland, possibly using this cave as a hideout. The thought comforted her; she had nothing to fear from the Wallners. She snorted at the irony: what had become of law and order when she feared the authorities more than those who deceived them?

Once her eyes had adjusted to the dim light inside the cave, she recognized the furnishings from past times: Against the wall stood the bench made of wooden boards, which Grandfather had so lovingly crafted. On it lay, neatly folded, two coarse horse blankets.

She smiled and reached behind a large stone where they had kept their treasure chest. Amazed, she pulled out the old tin box and opened the rusty lid. A yellowed Winnetou book, a flashlight with leaked batteries, some fossilized shells—everything was exactly as they had left it years ago.

Looking at the familiar items, tears came to her eyes, while at the same time a comforting warmth spread through her body. If her childhood treasures had survived, it must be a good omen for her own fate.

She took a notebook from her backpack, sat at the cave entrance and began to draw. Eventually a distant thunder startled her. Down in the valley, the sun was still shining, but behind the mountain peaks on the weather side, dark clouds were gathering. A storm would probably arrive by evening.

Anxiety prickled her skin; after all, she had learned from childhood on that thunderstorms in the mountains were dangerous. She closed her notebook with a sigh. While there was still enough light, she wanted to unpack her things and make the cave somewhat homey. If her childhood treasures had endured over the years, she too would be safe from the forces of nature within the cave.

CHAPTER 12

It was still dark outside when Astrid folded her nightgown. Once she was finished packing, she grabbed her backpack and descended the stairs to the guest room. Herr Weinberg was already sitting at the breakfast table with a steaming cup of ersatz coffee in front of him.

The innkeeper must have heard Astrid, because shortly afterward the door opened as she entered carrying a tray full of deliciously smelling items. Astrid's mouth watered as she watched the woman set the table with freshly baked bread and homemade quince jam in a preserving jar. As if that weren't enough of a feast, the innkeeper added a plate with one slice of smoked ham for each guest and a thumb-thick piece of hard cheese.

Astrid sent silent thanks to her mother, who had given her money and Aryan food ration cards. It had been ages since she'd eaten this well—fresh bread, real cheese, and even ham. She inhaled the delicious aroma emanating from the bread, her stomach doing somersaults in anticipation. "Did you bake this yourself?"

"No. I fetch it fresh every morning from the bakery down at the main square. The bakery belongs to my brother."

"It smells delicious," Astrid praised.

"It has rye and caraway in it." The landlady beamed with pride as she placed golden-yellow butter on the table and turned to Herr Weinberg. "Your wife hasn't arrived yet? Should I show her to the room once she comes?"

Herr Weinberg's face grew sad. "She hasn't called?"

"No, I'm sorry. No one has called."

"I'm very worried about my dear Martha. It's not like her to be late. I'm afraid something has happened to her. For this reason, my niece and I will unfortunately have to depart today."

Astrid nearly choked on her coffee at the unexpected family relationship.

"Are you sure? You've already paid half-board for today."

Again, Herr Weinberg nodded sadly. "Quite sure. I blame myself terribly for not traveling together. My dear Martha insisted on visiting her cousin first, and unfortunately, I couldn't get away from business any earlier."

"You shouldn't worry yourself. I'm sure the constant train delays are to blame."

"Still, I'm very concerned. My wife's health is not the best. I should never have let her travel alone."

"I'm terribly sorry." The landlady seemed inconsolable until her expression brightened. "You know what? Instead of dinner, I'll prepare a hearty lunch package for you. You have a long journey ahead to Vienna."

"Thank you, that would be incredibly kind of you." Herr Weinberg gazed at her with adoring eyes.

"I'm happy to do this, esteemed Herr Weinberg."

"I will praise your guesthouse in the highest terms to my business partners. Hopefully my wife and I can return in the spring to visit your wonderful area."

Astrid perked up her ears. The man truly played the piano of appearances with virtuoso skill. She could learn a thing or two from him.

"I wish you a safe journey home. I'm sure you'll find your wife there, safe and sound."

"My most heartfelt thanks once again."

After breakfast, they retrieved their belongings from their rooms and checked out at the reception, where the innkeeper handed them each a huge brown paper bag with provisions.

"Once again, my most humble thanks for your kindness. The stay at your guesthouse has been utterly delightful." Herr Weinberg extended his hand to the landlady and gazed at her adoringly, leaving the woman melting under his charm.

"Don't mention it, Herr Weinberg. It's the least I can do for you."

"Thank you so much for the provisions. We'll definitely return someday," Astrid added her thanks. Once they had left the guesthouse, she said: "You handled that brilliantly, Herr Weinberg."

He smiled. "Please, call me by my first name. From now on, I'm your uncle and my name is Bruno."

Astrid felt herself blushing. "Bruno. By the way, I'm Astrid."

He raised an eyebrow. "Last night, your first name was Sieglinde."

"I... oh..." Astrid could have slapped herself for the faux pas. "It's... well... Sieglinde is the name on my passport."

"Then I should call you Sieglinde. One cannot be too careful."

"Thank you." Astrid made a contrite face. "I still have much to learn."

"I've been living underground for quite some time. The deceiving becomes second nature."

On the way to the arranged meeting point with the

smuggler, they encountered an older woman. "Are you going hiking today?"

Astrid was momentarily speechless with shock, but Bruno didn't hesitate for a second, answering kindly. "We'd like to explore the beautiful region."

"It's going to be a sunny day today." The woman glanced toward the mountain peaks. "Are you familiar with the area?"

"Don't worry, we'll stay on the well-marked paths. We're heading up to Grasjoch."

"That's a rewarding hike, not overly difficult." With that, the woman continued on her way.

Astrid whispered, "Did you know that woman?"

"I met her on the train." Bruno pushed his hat lower on his forehead. "I underestimated how closely people in the countryside watch strangers. In Vienna, nobody stops to talk to someone they don't know."

"Where I'm from... neither." Astrid bit her tongue just in time before she blurted out the name of her hometown. Though she had nothing to fear from Bruno, she didn't want to be reprimanded a second time for her loose lips.

"We need to disappear quickly, or people will start asking questions." He quickened his pace.

"Why did you tell her that we're going to Grasjoch? Now she knows where to find us."

Bruno kept looking straight ahead. "They won't find us at Grasjoch because we're not going there. It's on the other side of the valley. We want to go west, to Sankt Antönierjoch, where the border crossing to Switzerland is."

Astrid processed the information with wide eyes. "You... you truly have thought of everything, Bruno."

"I can't take the praise, since it was Karl's idea."

Euphoria rushed through Astrid's veins. The mysterious Karl seemed to live up to his reputation. After all he had safely guided Herr Jakobi's sons across the border. In the next moment a chill raced down her spine. "Do you think he'll take me along?"

"Why not? It shouldn't matter to him who he smuggles across the border."

Astrid wasn't so sure. Karl might suspect she was a Gestapo informant and refuse to take her. Another thought made her shudder. "How much does Karl charge anyway?"

"One thousand Reichsmarks per person."

"What?" Astrid stopped in her tracks. "I don't have that much money."

Bruno shook his head in thought. "Haven't you already been in contact with Karl?"

"No. He helped a couple of acquaintances some time ago." All hope drained from her body. It felt as if she were shrinking to the size of a Thumbelina.

Suddenly Bruno's face lit up. "It doesn't matter. The tour is already paid for. You can take Martha's place."

"That's not right," she protested weakly.

"Why not? Martha isn't here. The important thing is that the smuggler gets his money."

"What happens if Martha does show up and discovers someone else has taken the tour she paid for?" Astrid felt uneasy about snatching the woman's chance of escaping to freedom.

Bruno scratched his head. "I'm pretty sure she's been arrested."

"And if not?" she asked miserably.

He furrowed his brow. After a while, he said, "I have money in an account in Switzerland. I'll talk to Felix. If Martha shows up after all, I'll pay for her trip."

"You'd really do that?" Astrid nearly jumped for joy. "How can I ever repay you?"

"You don't have to. It's enough of a reward if we both

arrive safely in Switzerland. It would make me the happiest person in the world."

"Thank you," whispered Astrid. His generous offer had solved all her problems in one fell swoop, since she had spent her last cash at the guesthouse. Besides her mother's gold wedding ring, she owned nothing else of value.

At the arranged meeting point, a lean, weather-beaten man was waiting. He wore a gray jacket, a hat, knee-breeches, thick brown wool socks, and brown, impeccably polished mountain boots that looked strange at second glance. He studied Astrid and Bruno with watchful, light blue eyes.

Astrid self-consciously peered down at her own ill-fitting shoes.

"Good day. You must be Bruno and Martha?" the man greeted them in the region's thick Austrian accent.

Before Bruno could answer, Astrid stepped forward. "Something came up for Martha, so I'm taking her place. I'm Sieglinde."

The smuggler's expression darkened, and he growled: "That wasn't the arrangement."

"Please. There won't be any problems. The police don't know I'm here."

He stared at her with a look she couldn't decipher, about to answer when Bruno calmly said, "You were paid for two people. There are two of us."

The smuggler grumbled something unintelligible, then nodded briefly. "All right. I'm Felix. These are the rules: You do what I say—no questions. I've walked this route a thousand times; I know every stone. Anyone who deviates even one step from the plan will be left behind, because he puts us all in danger. Understood?"

A queasy feeling gathered in the pit of Astrid's stomach. "Understood."

"Good. This tour isn't a walk in the park. The march is

rough, many dangers await. Starting with the mountains, the weather, rock slides, all the way to the border police patrolling the area."

Astrid fought against the urge to throw up. Perhaps it wasn't such a good idea to flee to Switzerland across the Alps after all.

Felix fixed her with his gaze. "I'm not saying this to scare you, but to teach you respect. If you follow my instructions without objection, you'll find yourselves on the other side of the border by tonight. Understood?"

"Understood." Astrid tried to give her voice a firm tone. Felix might sound harsh, but she discerned kindness in his eyes. He seemed genuinely concerned for the well-being of his charges. Intuitively, she felt safe with him.

Bruno, on the other hand, grimaced. "I know what to expect. I'm familiar with the mountains."

"All the more reason to obey my orders. I determine what, how, and where we go, and I tolerate no objection." Felix took a step toward Bruno and planted himself squarely in front of him. It was a demonstration of power, the kind Astrid had often witnessed her brothers doing.

"Of course. You're the guide." Bruno took a step back, signaling that he acknowledged the other's superiority.

"One more thing. I go first. No one passes me, no matter what happens." Without waiting for an answer, Felix set off.

His pace was murderous. Even on level ground, Astrid had to exert herself to keep up. As soon as they started climbing the slope, she was gasping. The thin mountain air didn't fill her lungs with enough oxygen, so her heart was pumping like crazy. Sweating, she unbuttoned her jacket and fanned cool air onto her heated cheeks.

After less than twenty minutes, her calves and thighs ached with every laborious upward step; her toes pressed painfully together in her too-small shoes, and her left heel chafed against the stiff leather. A blister would surely form soon.

Moreover, she constantly slipped on the loose scree, barely catching herself. Each time, she lost valuable inches that she had to climb up again. She noticed with embarrassment that Felix and Bruno stopped every few minutes to wait for her. Even Bruno, who was significantly older, didn't seem to have much trouble with the brisk pace.

Her eyes fixated on her next step, she gasped with her mouth open until finally temporary relief came in the form of a flat stretch where the two men waited. Felix held out a bottle of water to her. The cool liquid ran down her dust-dry throat, refreshing her spirits. After a few minutes' rest, she said, "We can continue."

"Good," growled the smuggler, who in his surefootedness and speed resembled an ibex more than a human.

With endless relief, Astrid noticed he had slowed his pace. Or perhaps it just seemed that way because walking on flat terrain was so much easier than on the slope. She even found time to let her gaze sweep over the magnificent landscape.

Majestic snow-covered peaks rose up before her; to her right lay the valley, lined with green meadows, through which a glittering blue river meandered. She would have liked to pause and enjoy the view, but Felix drove the small group mercilessly forward—toward freedom.

Therefore she gritted her teeth, ignored her protesting muscles and fought her way forward one step at a time. She would not give up, no matter the cost. She owed it not only to herself but to her mother and her entire family.

CHAPTER 13

Felix stopped for the umpteenth time and gazed toward the western ridge, an uneasy feeling pooling in the pit of his stomach. He didn't like the black and threatening clouds piling up. He knew the weather signs in the mountains, and these promised nothing good.

At the next bend, he waited for his charges. Bruno was holding up well for his age, but this girl... Felix shook his head. She definitely wasn't made for the mountains. Her cheeks flushed by exhaustion, she struggled up the slope, panting and stumbling.

If he had been alone, he would already have arrived at the final ascent to the border hut. The two border guards currently on duty were willing, for an appropriate compensation, to turn a blind eye when illegal goods or people crossed the border. Due to Sieglinde, he wasn't moving half as fast as he'd estimated, which jeopardized the entire plan, because at exactly 6 PM the guards would change —and Felix didn't know where the night shift's loyalty lay.

Added to that came the danger of a storm breaking out

before they reached the pass. As if on cue, a distant rumble of thunder made him flinch.

"Holy Mother of God," he muttered, rubbing his chin. The thunderclouds gathering over the ridge seemed close enough to touch. The sensible thing would be to abort the mission and return to the village. He waited for his two charges. Sieglinde instantly flopped down on a large rock and took a sip from her water bottle.

Bruno, however, studied him attentively. "Is something wrong?"

"See those clouds up there? A storm is brewing."

Bruno nodded. "I've seen them too. They can still move the other direction."

Felix wrestled with himself. He didn't want to disappoint his charges, but he also had to ensure their safety. "We don't want to be caught by a thunderstorm in the open. We need to cancel the tour."

Sieglinde stared at him with wide, frightened eyes, her mouth hanging agape. Bruno, on the other hand, turned chalk-white and sank down on the rock next to her. "That's not possible. That would be our death."

"We'll try again as soon as the storm has passed. Until then, you can stay in the village."

"That's not possible," Bruno protested a second time in a weak voice. "We told the innkeeper we were returning to Vienna."

"Plans can change." Felix rubbed his chin.

"Because Martha didn't show up, Bruno told the innkeeper we were going to look for her. She'll definitely find it suspicious if we return without Martha and act as if nothing happened."

"Damn." Felix observed the dark clouds behind the ridge with squinted eyes. Although the possibility was low, they might drift in another direction or rain out before reaching the hikers.

If someone in the village became suspicious and reported Bruno and Sieglinde to the police, they weren't the only ones in trouble. He would likely be arrested too. No matter how he looked at it, both alternatives were risky. If the Jews were caught, they would soon share the fate of those betrayed in early summer and swing from the gallows, possibly alongside Felix.

Even if he somehow managed to wriggle himself out of jail, their blood would be on his hands. He shook his head. Under these circumstances, he preferred the mountains. First, he knew the dangers, and second, nature wasn't out to destroy him.

"All right, we'll continue. But we need to pick up the pace." After another ten minutes, a loud "Ouch!" rang out. Startled by the cry, he turned around just in time to see Sieglinde fall and slide several meters down the slope. At the sound her knee made when it hit a rock, he winced in shock. *Just what we need!*

She got up surprisingly quick, but even from a distance, her pain-contorted grimace was unmistakable as she put weight on her foot. In a few large strides, he was beside her and asked, against his better judgment, "Everything all right?"

"I think so," she grunted.

"Can you continue?"

"Certainly. I have to," she pressed out between clenched jaws.

One had to give the young woman credit: she might not be an experienced mountaineer, but she certainly possessed enough fighting spirit for two.

"We'll take a short break. Sit down," he ordered and handed her the water bottle.

Gratitude brought a smile to her pained face. She drank greedily several gulps, before handing the bottle back. While Sieglinde and Bruno caught their breath, Felix moved a few steps away from the path until he found what he was looking for: a long stick Sieglinde could lean on while walking.

"Get up," he commanded, held the stick to her side and broke it off above her hip. "Use this to support yourself when walking. It will take pressure off your damaged knee and give you stability."

"Thank you." She was still panting. "I'm sorry."

"Don't worry about it. But now we must continue." Another rumble of thunder sounded, closer than before. Felix took the lead of the small group and urged: "We have to hurry."

After another twenty minutes of climbing, Felix felt a raindrop on his nose. The next section was flatter, yet it offered no shelter from rain, storm or lightning strikes. It would be downright foolish to stay in the open if the storm broke out. They needed safe shelter, and fast.

He scanned the terrain that he knew like the back of his hand. As his gaze swept over a row of low rocks located several hundred meters away, the corners of his mouth turned up. Hidden in that rock formation was a cave. His nephews had discovered it years ago, playing with village children from Gargellen; this summer, a deserter fleeing the Nazis had spent the night, before the young shepherd found him and guided him across the border.

The cave lay in the opposite direction to their destination. In their current predicament, Felix didn't care about a delay. It was more important to ride the storm out in a dry place that offered good protection.

"A change of plan," he announced, pointing to the rock formation. "Over there is a cave where we can weather the storm."

Bruno furrowed his brow. "How long will we be stuck in there?"

Felix shrugged. "Hard to say. Could be an hour, maybe three or four—depending on how long the thunderstorm lasts."

"Will we still make it to the border in time?"

The question hit a sore spot. As usual, Felix had insisted on setting out early in the morning, because he always factored in delays. Regardless, time was running short. If the tempest held them up for more than three hours, they would definitely not make it to the mountain pass before the guards changed. But he would worry about it when they came to it.

"We won't make it, will we?" Sieglinde groused in a pitiful voice.

"I can't guarantee that we'll reach the border today," Felix admitted honestly. "What I do know with absolute certainty is that we risk our lives if we don't seek shelter. You shouldn't underestimate a thunderstorm up here. In the worst case, we'll have to spend the night in the cave."

Bruno's Adam's apple bobbed up and down, but he remained silent. Sieglinde didn't utter another word either; on the contrary, relief spread across her face when she realized she might not have to march any further on that day.

"Let's go. It will take us about twenty minutes to reach the cave. We need to hurry if we don't want to get wet."

Despite being hit by occasional raindrops, Felix was in good spirits. They approached the cave in a steady, if slow, pace. Minutes before they reached their destination, the heavens opened the floodgates and poured buckets of water over them. Within a minute, Felix's hat and jacket were soaked through. His shirt clung cold and wet to his arms and shoulders. The wind whistled and howled.

"Bruno, you go first. See the rock over there? That's where

we need to go." He pointed in the direction. "Sieglinde walks in the middle, and I'll bring up the rear."

"Understood." Bruno nodded and set off again.

The pouring rain turned the path into a slippery trap, which was especially hard on Sieglinde. Her fingers clutched the walking stick so tightly that her knuckles turned white. Before each step with her injured knee, she hesitated a moment and seemed to search for a place to put her foot. She inevitably buckled when putting weight on it, slowing her pace down even more.

Her rigid posture revealed both pain and concentration. Felix was about to throw her over his shoulder and carry her the last few meters to the saving cave, when all hell broke loose around them.

The temperature had dropped at least fifteen degrees in the last few minutes. The storm whipped the rain horizontally ahead of it, the drops boring into Felix's face like pinpricks. He pulled his hat lower over his forehead, bracing himself against the wind with all his might. Lightning flashed across the dark sky. In his mind, Felix counted the seconds until he heard the thunder. *One, two, three, four, five*, crash.

The realization that the thunderstorm was almost two kilometers away let him breathe easier. Between the next flash and its thunder passed a mere three seconds.

Concern for himself and his charges ate deep into his bones. Startled by the deafening rumble, Sieglinde flinched and slipped on the muddy ground. Just in time, Felix jumped forward to prevent her from falling by grabbing her upper body.

"Come on, we have to keep going. It's not much further," he yelled against the roaring wind.

A jolt went through her body, and she moved toward the rock overhang, under which Bruno had sought shelter from the rain and wind. Two agonizing minutes later, they joined him under the protective roof.

Sieglinde bent forward, gasping heavily.

"Are you alright?" Felix asked.

"Yes, I... just... have... a... stitch... in my side."

Felix didn't actually expect to find an unpleasant surprise in the cave, but he still wanted to check whether the coast was clear. "Listen carefully. I'll scout ahead first; you wait here and come in once I call you."

Bruno nodded his consent; Sieglinde didn't seem to have listened, as she continued to bend forward, holding her sides.

Felix rummaged in his backpack for his flashlight, pushed aside the bramble bushes, and felt his way into the cave, where almost complete darkness reigned. Not a sound could be heard. He shone the light along the walls until the beam fell upon a figure pressed into a corner, apparently hoping not to be discovered.

"Don't be afraid. I won't hurt you!" Felix reassured the person, whom he recognized as a young woman. Her face seemed vaguely familiar.

She examined him, until her lips pursed. "Are you... Felix Wallner? The notorious smuggler?"

"That's me." Against his will, a proud grin spread from ear to ear. "It seems my reputation precedes me. And who are you?"

"I prefer to remain anonymous."

"So you're on the run from the law."

A barely perceptible nod was the answer.

Felix chuckled. "I've never been particularly law-abiding. You don't need to be afraid; I won't tell on you."

She worried her lower lip, staring at him.

To dispel her mistrust, he said: "Many things are said about me; most of it isn't true. Though, you should know that

I can't stand the Nazis. Whatever you've done, I won't turn you over to the authorities."

Finally, her facial features relaxed. "I'm Bärbel, the granddaughter of the Eggers in Gargellen."

"You and your siblings were the children playing with my nephews in this cave?"

"Yes. I wanted to lay low here for a while until the police stop looking for me in the village."

To avoid arousing her suspicion again, Felix refrained from asking what she had done. She definitely wasn't Jewish. He cleared his throat: "I have two friends with me who want to go to Switzerland. May they come in?"

Bärbel's mouth fell open and closed again. Then she nodded.

He returned to the entrance of the cave and waved his charges inside. "We're staying here for now; another woman has sought shelter in the cave. Don't worry. She won't betray us; she's very anti-Nazi. Her name is Bärbel."

The two followed the beam of his flashlight into the cave. The unexpected encounter with Bärbel had surprised Felix. His first reaction had been to leave without mentioning the refugees. On second thought, he'd changed his mind. Bärbel was herself on the run from the authorities, and his gut feeling told him she posed no danger. Regardless, he resolved to be on his guard.

Sieglinde and Bruno had followed him inside. Exhaustion was written all over their faces. Especially Sieglinde was trembling in her dripping wet clothes. She looked as if she could hardly stand up, let alone think clearly.

Bruno, on the other hand, put on a charming smile as soon as he spotted Bärbel. He extended his hand to her. "Madam, thank you so much for allowing us to shelter in here. It's a pleasure to keep such a charming woman company."

Bärbel was visibly smitten. "Why, certainly! Please, drop the formalities and let's use first names."

His eyes lit up. "Gladly, dear Bärbel. I'm Bruno."

Beside him stood Sieglinde with chattering teeth looking like a drowned rat. Her hair clung to her head in wet strands and a puddle formed around her feet. She extended her hand to Bärbel. "My name is Astrid."

"Please, make yourselves at home." Bärbel made a welcoming gesture.

Felix, on the other hand, made a mental note to have a word with the young woman later. He didn't care whether she called herself Sieglinde or Astrid, but she needed to stick to one name.

In the light of Felix's flashlight, Bärbel went into a corner and lit a candle, which she must have blown out when she heard Felix coming. The flame cast eerie shadows on the wall while simultaneously managing to create a cozy atmosphere in the sparse room.

"You're soaking wet!" Bärbel said.

"The downpour caught us a few minutes before we reached the entrance to the cave." Felix took off his drenched jacket and hung it on Sieglinde's—or Astrid's?—stick, which leaned against the wall.

"Wait a moment." Bärbel rummaged in her backpack and pulled out a thick wool sweater and a pair of long underwear, which she gave to Astrid. "Here, put these on. Otherwise, you'll catch your death." She pointed to a dark corner of the cave. "You can change over there."

"Thank you." With trembling fingers, Astrid took the dry clothes and limped to the corner.

"What's wrong with your knee?" Bärbel asked.

"I fell. I don't think anything's broken, but it hurts like hell."

"As soon as you've changed, I'll take a look at it."

"Do you know something about first aid?" Felix asked.

"I'm a medical student." A hard line appeared around her mouth, signaling to Felix that he should refrain from asking further questions.

While Astrid changed in the corner, Bruno struggled out of his soaked jacket. Underneath, a mostly dry shirt emerged.

"Not all bad," Bruno muttered.

Felix too took off his soaked shirt, mentally considering their options.

"May I offer you a blanket?" Bärbel interrupted his thoughts, pointing to two gray horse blankets neatly folded on the wooden bench.

"Thank you." He didn't feel cold. Regardless, he draped a blanket around his shoulders. "I'll check on the weather." Outside, the situation hadn't improved. The storm continued with undiminished force; lightning flashed across the dark gray sky, thunder following practically in the same instant.

Glad to have found shelter from the elements in the cave, he returned inside, where the three people had settled next to each other on the bench, eating their provisions. Felix squatted on the floor in front of the bench and pulled a thick piece of bread with ham from his backpack. As soon as he had washed down the first bite with water from his flask, it suddenly occurred to him that they hadn't packed provisions for another day.

Bärbel offered an apple to everyone, which he declined. "You need the food yourself; I'll manage." It wouldn't be the first time he went hungry for a few days. Besides, he could buy provisions from the border guards up at the pass.

After they had finished eating, Bärbel said, "Let me examine your knee, Astrid."

Felix watched with interest as she diligently palpated the swollen area. Several times Astrid winced.

"Nothing's broken and the tendons seem intact too.

However, there's a large bruise forming, which is causing the pain when you walk."

"At least it's not serious," Astrid pressed out between clenched jaws.

Bärbel retrieved something that looked like an undershirt from her backpack, dampened it with water she wrung from the wet jackets and tied it around Astrid's knee. "The cold will reduce the swelling as well as numb the pain."

Outside the wind howled viciously. Now and then, a particularly violent gust rushed into the cave, causing the candlelight to flicker. Nonetheless, Felix maintained a glimmer of hope that the storm would soon pass. Every ten minutes or so, he walked to the entrance to survey the situation.

The storm had put them in a precarious position. If they wanted to reach the border at St. Antönier Pass in time before the change of guards, they would have to hurry. But the lashing rain and low-hanging clouds dashed his hopes. He was standing under the protective overhang next to the entrance when a bright flash of lightning streaked across the sky at the same time a thunderclap rumbled. His ears rang from the deafening noise, even before it echoed a dozen times off the mountains.

It would have been irresponsible to attempt the ascent. Meanwhile it was afternoon, and soon dusk would set in. Even if the rain subsided, it was suicide to attempt the steep climb to the pass in the dark with two mountain novices. Given Sieglinde's damaged knee, the bribed border guards would have finished their shift by the time they finally arrived up there anyway.

Reluctantly, Felix decided to weather the night in the cave. He took Bärbel aside. "I'm sorry, but we probably have to spend the night here. If you don't mind..."

Her eyes shone with understanding. "I almost expected that. Of course I don't mind; besides, it's not my cave."

"Thank you. Tomorrow the world will surely look much better."

"Hopefully by then the swelling in Astrid's knee will have gone down."

"Thanks again for your help."

"You're welcome." She looked at him with a tilted head. "People in Gargellen call you the Jew smuggler."

Felix waved it off. "People talk a lot. It's no secret how my family has earned its money for generations."

"Personally, I admire what you do."

Her answer shamed him. Initially, he had done these tours solely for the money—before he realized what happened to Jews who didn't leave the German Reich in time.

After his conversation with Bärbel, he took Sieglinde aside. "Listen to me."

"I'm sorry, the name just slipped out," she preempted his lecture.

"I don't care what you call yourself, as long as you always use the same name. Anything else leads to confusion, suspicion and ultimately your arrest."

She looked at him with wide eyes. "What should I do?"

Inwardly, Felix shook his head at such naivety. "Since you claimed to Bärbel that your name is Astrid, you'd better stick with it."

The tension dissolved from her expression. "That is my real name, anyway."

"I don't want to know." He raised his hands in defense. "For your protection and mine, I don't want to know anything about you or your past. I'll take you to the border; after that, we'll never see each other again."

"Understood. And thank you for everything." She looked as if she wanted to say something else, but clenched her jaw.

It was probably for the best. Too much information could prove fatal.

Later, as Felix lay next to Bruno on the ground, wrapped together in a horse blanket—the two women sharing the second one—he considered the various routes for the next day. Under normal circumstances he would take the shorter route over the steep slope, but with Astrid's knee, it might be advisable to take the longer, technically less challenging route around the ridge.

He sighed, tabling the decision for the next morning. His only hope was that the storm would disperse as quickly as it had gathered, and that the sun would shine again from the sky in the morning.

CHAPTER 14

Bärbel lay under the scratchy blanket she shared with Astrid, listening to the howling storm. Although she was tired, she couldn't find sleep. Her thoughts constantly circled around the day's events. Next to her, Astrid seemed to have the same problem.

"Can't you sleep either?" Bärbel whispered.

"My knee is throbbing horribly."

"Stick it out from under the blanket so it can cool down."

Astrid moved with a groan. "Much better."

"How did that happen anyway?"

"I slipped and fell. You know," Astrid hesitated, "I've never been in the mountains before. It's all unfamiliar to me and much more strenuous than I expected."

Bärbel turned toward her. "It's pretty brave of you to attempt such a difficult journey on your first trip."

"More desperate than brave." Bitterness laced Astrid's voice. "I don't know how I'll make it up to the pass tomorrow."

"You'll manage. Felix knows every stone in the region; he'll get you to the border."

After a pause, Astrid asked, "Are you also... I mean, are you Jewish?"

"No. You won't tell the police about me, will you?"

"Me? Even if I wanted to, nobody would listen to me—they'd just drag me straight to a concentration camp."

"It's terrible to see what has become of our country since the Anschluss." Bärbel paused. The danger of Astrid reporting her was minimal, it was a great opportunity to get everything off her chest. "I distributed White Rose leaflets."

Astrid sharply inhaled. "The student group from Munich? I heard about them. All the members were..."

"Executed. Yes." Bärbel had to clear her throat before she could continue. "Sentenced by Judge Roland Freisler at the People's Court."

"A dreadful man," Astrid whispered. "They say he mocks the defendants in the courtroom."

"He does. He scolds, shouts, insults, tears people apart. He's one of the worst representatives of the Nazi regime. His trials are pure spectacle, the verdict determined long before the accused even enter the courtroom." Bärbel swallowed the lump in her throat. "I read every newspaper article about the trials. It was almost unbearable. Especially because Christoph Probst..." Her voice broke; she needed several seconds to compose herself. "He and I became friends when he transferred to the University of Innsbruck last year."

"I'm so sorry." Astrid gently stroked her shoulder. "So much grief and death wherever you look."

"When the Gestapo arrested fellow students of ours, I got scared and fled Innsbruck." Bärbel closed her eyes, trapped in her worrisome thoughts. Outside, the rain pattered, on the other side of the cave one of the men was snoring. Eventually, she fell asleep.

A scraping sound jolted Bärbel from her restless sleep. Her hips and shoulders ached due to lying on the hard cave floor. By her side Astrid breathed calmly and evenly. In the gray dawn light, she noticed that Felix's spot was empty. Just Bruno lay there, his chest rising and falling steadily.

To avoid waking the others, she quietly slipped out from under the warm blanket and walked to the cave entrance, where she made out Felix's silhouette. A glowing point danced in the air, seconds later the aroma of a cigarette wafted into her nose.

Once she reached him, the sight took her breath away. "Good heavens!"

"Good morning to you too," chuckled Felix, his breath forming steam clouds in the icy morning air, which rivaled the cigarette smoke.

"When did this happen?" Overnight, at least twenty inches of snow had fallen. Glistening white, untouched fresh snow covered the mountain landscape like powdered sugar. The rising sun poured its rays over the ridge, bathing the peaks in a red-gold light.

Felix scratched the back of his head. "This is a disaster. I certainly don't need this freaking snow."

Usually Bärbel liked snow, because it looked so pretty when the mountains rose with white whipped cream tops against the blue sky. In their current situation though, she shared Felix's opinion; the snow was a catastrophe. Nonetheless she tried to reassure him, "You've surely experienced winter weather on the trail before. You can handle it, right?"

"I can," he confirmed grimly, nodding toward the cave. "Not so sure about the other two, especially Astrid with her swollen knee."

"I'm confident the swelling has gone down overnight. In any case, she should keep the knee cool, which should be easy considering the fresh snow." Bärbel was already thinking where she could tear off a piece of cloth, as she didn't want to give up her undershirt.

"It's not just that." His weather-beaten forehead wrinkled with worry. "In fresh snow, every footprint stands out like a neon sign."

An icy shiver, having nothing to do with the cold temperature, raced down Bärbel's spine. "Do you believe the Gestapo is searching for them?"

He shrugged. "I don't think so. At the guesthouse, Bruno told the innkeeper that they had to return to Vienna early."

"Thank goodness." At least that danger seemed averted.

"In any case, both of them need to leave the country as soon as possible." He kicked at the snow, frustration evident in his movements. "We need to get up to Sankt Antönier Pass, but we can't take the direct route over the ridge. Without crampons, it's life-threatening in these conditions." He gazed at her. "I'm sorry if we've caused you any inconvenience."

Bärbel took a deep breath. She had thought about the idea half the night, and she would hardly get a better opportunity to ask him the question burning in her soul. "Could you take me with you... I mean to the border?"

Felix took a drag from his cigarette before drawling, "I was paid for two people, not three."

"Please." She would have thrown herself into the snow at his feet if she believed it would convince him. "The winter weather has made my situation difficult. I can't go to my grandmother's for food without my footprints being visible."

He observed her for a few seconds, rubbing his unshaved face. "How good are you at mountain climbing? I can't handle another person I need to look after."

Confidence spread through Bärbel's bones. "I spent most of my school holidays in Gargellen, practically grew up in the mountains. I definitely won't be a burden; on the contrary, I can help you with Astrid."

"Alright then." His voice sounded resigned. "But at your own risk. I can't guarantee anything."

"Thank you so much."

"Don't thank me yet. Whether you'll be able to cross into Switzerland depends exclusively on the border guards, who are expecting two people. I assume they'll demand extra payment."

His words hit her like a cold shower. "I don't have money."

"Then I don't see much of a chance." He looked at her with pity. "They don't do this out of kindness, but pure greed."

Desperately, Bärbel racked her brain for a solution, until she remembered her necklace. She reached for the pendant, a silver cross, showing it to Felix. "I have this silver necklace."

He examined the piece of jewelry with skeptical eyes. "That's probably not enough, but we can try."

"And if they don't let me pass?"

"Then you'll have to return."

Bärbel wasn't thrilled at the prospect of making the journey from the pass to the cave on her own, yet she nodded anyway. Secretly, she hoped the border guards would be satisfied with the necklace.

"We should wake the others; the ascent will be arduous." Felix disappeared into the cave, while Bärbel stayed outside a few more minutes, peering down toward the valley where her grandmother lived.

"Grandma, I'm going to Switzerland. Take good care of yourself. I hope we'll see each other again after the war," she whispered before following Felix into the cave.

It didn't take long until everything was packed, and everyone had eaten an apple and several pieces of zwieback. Bärbel packed the remaining provisions so they had a snack during the journey.

They gathered in front of the entrance as Felix explained the plan for the day. "The fresh snow has changed the situation." He pointed to an untouched, white slope in front of them. "That's the direct route, but without proper equipment, we can't make it up there. We'll have to go around."

Bärbel looked in the direction he indicated. She knew the slope and was confident she could make it to the ridge even without crampons. The same probably couldn't be said for Bruno, and especially Astrid with her injured knee. Felix was acting responsibly to choose the longer route, even if that meant four or five more hours of walking time.

She shivered. In case of an accident, they couldn't count on rescue by the mountain patrol, as they would just hand them over to the police, which inevitably meant concentration camp or immediate execution.

At the absurdity of it, she shook her head: The Nazis spared neither expense nor effort to ensure they could properly deliver the rescued to the executioner.

CHAPTER 15

Astrid looked with apprehension at the landscape. Under different circumstances, she would have delighted in the sight of this winter wonderland. Today, however, her only thought was to make it safely up to the pass and into Switzerland.

"I'll make the trail, you step exactly in my footprints," Felix announced. "If a patrol discovers our tracks, they won't be able to tell how many people we are."

Astrid's eyes widened. She would never have thought of that. As the experienced mountaineer slogged, breaking a path through the deep snow, Astrid walked directly behind him, gratefully placing her smaller shoes into his large footprints.

Leaning on her walking stick, she looked neither left nor right. Her jaws clenched, she concentrated exclusively on stepping into Felix's footprints as precisely as possible without slipping. Her knee hurt less than she had feared— perhaps due to the cold, which was numbing it. Or because they were crossing a relatively flat area. Or simply because her fear pushed all other sensations into the background.

Since no one spoke, the crunching of their steps in the snow and the rhythmic breathing were the only sounds. In front of her, Felix's back moved up and down like clockwork. The march seemed to cause him no difficulty, even though he must be well over fifty.

She was grateful for the slow pace that allowed her to keep up without becoming overwrought. After a while, she relaxed. Her brain seemed to have internalized the movements, and she was able to occasionally risk a glance at the spectacular landscape.

As she took her next step, she hesitated. Felix's footprint somehow looked strange. She blinked. It was a print like any other and yet something was different. The glittering snow crystals reflected the blazing sunlight, blinding her. She would have loved to stop and examine the footprint more closely. Alas, that wasn't possible.

Without thinking further about it, she focused once more on her steps. Putting one foot in front of the other, she counted in her head the meters that brought her closer to freedom. Bruno marched directly behind her.

"I have cold feet. My socks are soaked through," he complained.

"That's tough," said Bärbel, coming up as the rear guard. "Do you have another pair of socks with you?"

"Yes, I do," he grumbled.

"Later, when we take a break put them on. But before you slip into your shoes afterward, you have to switch back to your wet socks."

"Oh really? How is that supposed to help?"

"That way you'll at least have one dry pair."

Astrid admired the other woman for her calm and thoughtful manner. The cooling knee bandage had worked wonders; her knee barely hurt anymore. This morning, Bärbel had taken good care of her, she had even torn off a piece of her own shirt to use as a bandage. Hopefully, Astrid could someday return the kindness.

An hour later, the sun burned on her back. Despite the overnight drop in temperature, she began to sweat from the unaccustomed movement. Not wanting to slow down the group, she didn't dare to stop and rummage in her backpack for her water bottle. Eventually, she couldn't withstand the thirst anymore. She grabbed a handful of snow with her bare hands and put it into her mouth. The cold hurt her teeth, but the refreshing relief as the melted snow ran down her throat definitely made up for it.

Distracted, she didn't pay attention, slipped, and had to support herself with her hand in the snow. After struggling back to her feet, her fingers stung from the cold. Gloves would have been useful. Unfortunately she hadn't thought about packing them when she'd left Frankfurt in temperatures of around fifteen degrees Celsius. But she didn't complain. Anything was better than being arrested, "suicided" or sent to a concentration camp and shot while allegedly trying to escape.

After the meager breakfast, it didn't take long for her stomach to growl its dissatisfaction with the lack of food. By the position of the sun high in the cloudless sky, she could tell it must be nearly noon. As if Felix had read her thoughts, he stopped next to a surprisingly warm rocky outcrop sheltered from the wind.

"We'll rest here," he announced. "Drink your water. Once the bottles are empty, fill them with snow, which will melt inside."

Astrid sank down onto a large stone, grateful for the break. Her legs trembled from the exertion. More urgent than something to drink, she needed food, but she had eaten the remains of the innkeeper's generous lunch package this morning. Just a single apple was left.

Next to her, Bruno pulled off his soaked shoes and socks, grumbling. He wrung out the socks and laid them in the sun to dry. Curiously, Astrid peeked at his pale toes, wrinkled from the moisture.

Once he noticed, he wiggled his toes. "It feels good to be out of those wet things."

"Soon we'll cross the border, and all of this will be forgotten." She cast him an encouraging smile, even though her own feet, covered in blisters, were causing her hellish pain.

Bärbel settled next to them and produced an astonishing amount of food from her backpack. Just the sight of it made Astrid's mouth water.

"Help yourselves," Bärbel invited them.

"Those are your provisions," Astrid protested.

"We're all in this together, so please, help yourselves."

Astrid didn't need to be asked a third time. She snatched several pieces of zwieback, handing one to each person. Bärbel cut a few pieces from the hard cheese, generously distributing them as well.

"Thank you. I'm starving." Bruno devoured the food. "This is delicious."

Felix had also joined them and stretched out his feet. Perplexed Astrid stared at his shoe soles.

"Tonight you'll be in Switzerland," Felix said as he chewed. "There you'll receive a warm meal."

"They're backward," said Astrid.

Bärbel looked at her, seemingly not comprehending. "What is backward?"

"The shoe soles." Astrid pointed to the brown leather boots on Felix's feet. "The toe is pointing backward."

The old man chuckled. "Did you notice that just now?"

"The entire time I thought something looked strange."

Bärbel laughed. "It's an old smuggler's trick. The sole is

nailed on the wrong way to mislead pursuers. If a customs officer follows fresh tracks in the snow, he walks away from the smuggler, not after him."

"How clever!" Astrid was impressed.

"Felix is a legend in the region. As children, my brothers and I often played smugglers and customs officers. Each of us wanted to be Felix Wallner." Bärbel's face took on a wistful expression. "Those were the days."

"Enough chatting, we have a long march ahead of us." Felix gave the signal to depart.

Astrid would have liked to sit in the sun a little longer, listening to Bärbel's stories, but the thought of a roof over her head and a hearty soup in Switzerland gave her the strength to stand up. Her injured knee throbbed uncomfortably, reminding her of its presence.

"One moment, I'm going to renew the bandage." As the others packed up and meticulously erased all traces of their presence from the resting place, Astrid removed the makeshift bandage, dipped it in the snow and wrapped it around her knee again. She grimaced, as the cold stung her skin. "Whew, that's cold!"

"You'll get used to it in a few moments; as long as the snow numbs the pain," Bärbel reassured her.

"It really does. Thank you again. Without you and your help, I couldn't have continued our journey."

"Then it was twice as fortunate that you took shelter in the smuggler's cave of all places."

"There aren't that many caves up here," Felix remarked.

Astrid noticed the impatient glare in his eyes and hurried to shoulder her backpack. "I'm ready."

They lined up again, and continued in a single file.

CHAPTER 16

Sweat streamed down Felix's face and back in rivulets as he laboriously took one step after another. The fresh snow was treacherous—a thin crust on top, wet and yielding underneath. At each step, he broke through, sinking knee-deep into the heavy mass that refused to release his foot.

Breaking trail was exhausting, more than he wanted to admit. Experience and endurance couldn't make up for his lost youthful vigor. Thirty years ago, he would have bounded up here as nimbly as a mountain goat; today, he felt his age with every step, deep into his bones.

Behind him, his charges were panting. Astrid was doing surprisingly well after the difficulties she'd had the day before. Bruno, however, struggled for secure footing in his city-fine leather shoes, which worried Felix. The man constantly slipped, each time struggling harder to get back up.

A cloudless blue sky was enthroned above the snow-covered peaks. On any other day, Felix would have enjoyed the mountain landscape to the fullest, might even have stopped to admire the view. Today though, the responsibility for three strangers' lives weighed heavily on his shoulders. The thunderstorm had literally thrown his plans into disarray, turning the journey more laborious and dangerous. Additionally, time was breathing down his neck. The longer they were on the move, the more could go wrong.

Someone would eventually notice the fugitives' absence and start asking questions. Then it wouldn't take a genius to connect them to Felix.

They rounded a rock formation. Behind it opened a magnificent view of an exposed valley.

"Beautiful," sighed Astrid, who was directly behind him.

"Unfortunately," grumbled Felix. In these perfect conditions one could see all the way down to Sankt Gallenkirch, which meant that an observer with binoculars could spot their four dark figures against the slope, too. Therefore he wanted to get past the exposed area as quickly as possible.

"We're changing the order," he decided. "Bruno takes the second spot, Astrid behind him and Bärbel last." This way he had Bruno, the weakest member of the group, within his reach and could intervene if necessary.

The group complied with the new arrangement without complaint. Bärbel just raised an eyebrow and assessed Bruno with a long look. She had probably noticed the man's diminishing stamina.

In retrospect, bringing Bärbel along proved to be a stroke of luck. She helped wherever she could. Her self-assessment hadn't been exaggerated; she was sure-footed and quick. If it had been just her and himself, Felix would have taken the direct route over the ridge.

"Let's continue," he ordered after the group had reformed. The path led along the edge of the valley where the snow was deeper and progress more strenuous; however, the cover was better. To give Bruno's smooth shoes a better grip, Felix stomped several times into each step until the loose snow compacted. After just a few minutes, his thighs protested against the exertion.

Since giving up wasn't an option, he ignored the pain and continued. His thoughts wandered far ahead, to the border, to the guards. Meinhold and Christoph were corruptible, but they hated surprises. He had told them to expect two refugees, not three.

Bärbel's silver necklace wasn't valuable enough for them to turn a blind eye. He would suggest paying the remaining amount next time. The question was whether they would agree to it.

Felix wiped the sweat from his forehead and turned around to the group. "Everything all right with you?"

Three nodding faces answered him. They looked exhausted, yet determined. Thus he trudged on, intent on covering the approximately four hours to the pass as quickly as possible.

A dull thud and a suppressed cry of pain made Felix spin around. Bruno lay helplessly on the ground.

"Damn snow!" Bruno hissed, making no attempt to get up. "If I had known this, I never would have come. It's early October, why the sudden onset of winter? This is a damn…"

Astrid extended her hand to help him up, but Bruno didn't seem to notice. Anger flashing in his eyes, he snarled, "I'm going to stay here until this murderous shit melts."

Felix took a deep breath. A stubborn, panicking man was the last thing he needed. In a soothing voice, he tried to persuade him: "Bruno, it's not much further. You can make it."

Bruno shook his head obstinately. "I'm not a little child! Of course it's still far! How long do we have to trudge across this stupid slope?"

"We've already managed more than half of it." At this moment, Felix wished his sister were here. Valentina knew how to bring tantrum-throwing children—or in this case, a full-grown man—back to their senses.

"Let the Gestapo catch me. It can't be worse than this slippery nightmare."

"You don't mean that," Astrid interjected, extending her walking stick toward Bruno. "Here, take this, it will give you stability."

Her generous offer seemed to make Bruno realize how childishly he was behaving. Felix could have hugged her. It took a few seconds, during which Bruno stared into the valley, before he said quietly, "Thank you, but I can't accept that. You need the stick yourself."

"Of course you can have it. My shoes have a tread, I hardly slip." That was a lie, as she too was struggling.

"And your knee?"

"It's much better thanks to Bärbel's cold compresses. Please, take the stick."

Finally Bruno grabbed it, and sure enough, with the support he regained stability and surefootedness. However, he carefully tested the ground each time before shifting his weight onto the next step.

Felix cast a worried glance at his wristwatch. He wanted to reach the pass in good time so he could make it home before dark. The thought of being stuck up there, where he would be at the mercy of the customs officers—whose favor he would have to buy at a high price—sent a shiver down his spine.

A few minutes later, Bruno fell again. Fortunately the stick prevented him from sliding down the slope. Felix suppressed a curse. This tour was turning into a full-blown nightmare. His teeth clenched, he trudged on, trying to find a pace that Bruno could manage without losing too much valuable time.

The next half hour passed in agonizing slowness. Bruno's panting grew louder by the minute, interrupted by muttered curses whenever he slipped. Felix forced himself to stay calm. Panic wouldn't help anyone.

After another near-fall, he ordered a short rest. "Drink something and eat a bite."

"How much further is it?" Bruno asked in a tense voice.

Usually he would need about two hours from here to the pass, but nothing about this journey was normal. "An hour at most," Felix lied, fearing the truth would trigger another defiant fit from Bruno. "There's less snow up ahead."

That was only half the truth. Felix didn't mention that the slope was too steep for snow to stay on it. He pushed aside the thought of the difficult stretch ahead of them. Instead, he studied his group. Astrid was holding up surprisingly well. Meanwhile she walked more securely without the stick than Bruno did with it. Bärbel seemed to have no problems at all; she hadn't lied about her mountain experience.

Shortly before they reached the steep section, Felix heard another slip, this time followed by a suppressed sob. Bruno had managed to stay standing, but the despair in his eyes was heartbreaking. The man had reached the end of his physical and emotional strength.

"Short break," Felix commanded. They really couldn't afford another delay. But if Bruno collapsed, it would take even longer. "Five minutes."

The steep slope rose before them like a white wall. Bruno turned pale as he looked up.

"We'll go up in zigzags. It's less strenuous." Felix waited until everyone had drunk before urging his group: "We need to continue."

He couldn't shake his worry about Bruno. The man who had been so self-confident yesterday seemed consumed by fear. His movements were stiff and clumsy. Felix stomped the steps especially carefully into the snow while encouraging the Viennese man. "Simply follow in my footprints. It's no different than yesterday."

"Except for this blasted snow..." Bruno panted.

They worked their way up in laborious serpentines to about halfway up the slope when a scream tore through the air. Felix spun around. Bruno was sliding down the slope on his stomach.

"Pull your elbows to your body and push them up!" Felix shouted.

Bruno didn't listen. Helplessly, Felix watched as the man continued to slide downward. The seconds passed as if in slow motion. Bruno slid wildly further and further until a rock jutting out of the snow about fifty meters below Felix's position stopped his forward momentum.

"Bruno!" Astrid's panicked scream echoed off the mountain walls.

Bärbel pressed her hand over her mouth in horror.

The fall had happened in the worst possible location: they stood exposed in the middle of the slope, visible from afar to potential pursuers. Cold sweat dripped from Felix's forehead as Bruno failed to respond even after repeated calls. His body lay motionless in the snow.

Felix's thoughts raced. If Bruno was injured... if he was unconscious... if he... No, he couldn't entertain this idea. What was he supposed to do? He couldn't leave the women alone in the middle of the slope. On the other hand, he had to get down to Bruno. Meanwhile, every minute they stood on display increased the danger of being discovered.

After a brief consideration, he instructed Bärbel: "I'll go down and check on Bruno; you and Astrid climb up to the ridge."

Bärbel shielded her eyes against the sun with her hand as she examined the slope. "We'll take steeper switchbacks, then we'll reach the top in fifteen minutes max. Can you manage, Astrid?"

Astrid was rather pale around the nose; however, she nodded bravely. "If you go first, then yes."

"If you're uncertain, go to the edge of the slope and wait for me there." Felix didn't want to pressure the two women into taking unnecessary risks. A second or third accident would be catastrophic.

"You don't need to worry about us. We'll manage just fine," Bärbel reassured him. "I've climbed slopes like this one a thousand times sledding with my brothers."

But Astrid hasn't, thought Felix. He bit his tongue and swallowed his doubts. "At the top of the ridge, wait for me on the leeward side; it's warmer there."

"Are you sure you don't need help with Bruno?" asked Bärbel, who seemed remarkably calm. She was securing a loose strand of hair with a hairpin into her bun, as if standing in front of a mirror rather than in the middle of a mountain.

For a moment, Felix was tempted to accept her offer. A second pair of hands would certainly be useful if Bruno was injured. Then he shook his head. "I'll climb down alone. If I need help, I'll signal you."

She gave him an encouraging smile. "There's no reason to worry about us. I'll take good care of Astrid."

"Thank you."

Bärbel turned to Astrid. "Come on. Let's go."

Felix watched a few seconds as they climbed up the slope. Bärbel seemed very confident, which transferred to Astrid, who stepped directly into her tracks. Sighing, Felix turned around. He had a queasy feeling letting the women climb up alone, but he had no choice.

As quickly as possible, he descended the slope, careful not to start sliding himself. After a few minutes, he approached Bruno, who lay curled up next to the rock. Expecting the worst, Felix's heart skipped a beat. Just before he reached Bruno, he noticed the rising and falling of his chest. A wave of relief swept through Felix.

With large steps, he stepped toward the fallen man and knelt beside him. "Are you hurt?"

"Everything hurts," Bruno whimpered.

"Can you move your arms and legs?" At first glance, everything looked normal. Felix spotted neither blood nor dislocated limbs; Bruno probably had just suffered a few scrapes and a good scare.

Such a slide down a slope often looked more dangerous than it actually was. As long as the person didn't crash into an obstacle or get a limb caught somewhere, injuries were usually minor.

"I think so." Bruno moved, just to freeze mid-motion. "Cursed snow! I'll never make it! I'm staying here until it melts."

Felix signaled to Bärbel and Astrid, who had reached the ridge, that everything was all right. Bärbel signaled back letting him know they would sit down on the sunny side. At least he didn't have to worry about the two women anymore.

Somewhat reassured, he focused his efforts on the distraught man. "Bruno, listen to me carefully. You can't stay here. Who knows how long it will take for the snow to melt again."

"I won't take another step in this slippery hell. Not a single one."

Felix didn't know how to shake Bruno out of his state of shock. For lack of a better idea, he sighed, "Then I'll stay with you, and we'll wait together until the Gestapo picks us up."

The threat returned life into Bruno's eyes. He blinked frantically. Seconds later, the flame died out and he muttered, "There's no point anyway. Just give me the coup de grace!"

The absurd request hit Felix like a punch to the gut,

followed by stinging anger. What was Bruno thinking? He wasn't risking life and limb guiding Bruno across the mountains to Switzerland just to shoot him half-way through the journey! What did this fancy gentleman think?

The hot temper that had gotten Felix into trouble since childhood took possession of him. Like a burning fire, it ate through his veins, and surged up, displacing every other thought. Red mist appeared before his eyes. Just in time before he said or did something rash, he squeezed his eyes shut, taking several deep breaths of the clear mountain air.

The smell of freshly fallen snow filled his nose. The sun, warming his back, did the rest. The mist dissolved, the raging fire in his veins receding. Still, Felix needed a few more inhales until he had regained enough self-control to speak in a calm voice.

"Listen, Bruno. First, I don't have a gun with me, and second, I would never shoot a defenseless person. You can't give up. You're alive, you're not injured, and the Swiss border is within reach."

"I can't do it." Whimpering, Bruno rocked his upper body back and forth. "I should have stayed in Vienna and hidden there."

"The Gestapo would have tracked you down sooner or later. Besides, it's pointless to question your decision. You're here, not in Vienna." Felix was becoming impatient. They urgently needed to leave the slope. If they were unlucky, Bruno's scream had alerted the policemen who constantly patrolled the region for illegal border crossers.

"Let them arrest me. Maybe the camps aren't as bad as their reputation." Stubborn as a child, Bruno pushed out his lower lip.

"On the contrary, they are even much worse than we can imagine." There was plenty of gossip in the village. Felix believed less than half of it, but even that was enough to chill his blood. "Give me your hand. I'll help you up."

"I'd rather die here." Despite his remark, Bruno held out a hand.

Felix grabbed it, horrified by the ice-cold fingers that felt like those of a corpse. He remembered people in shock, lowered all bodily functions to such an extent that their limbs often suffered diminished blood circulation. Felix wished Bärbel were standing beside him; in her medical studies, she must have learned what to do in case of shock. He risked looking up to the ridge. There was no sign of the women.

Since he couldn't think of a better idea, he rubbed Bruno's fingers until they took on a rosy color. The entire time, he spoke reassuring words. "You can do it. For sure. I'll always be with you. Up on the ridge, Bärbel and Astrid are waiting for us. Tonight you'll be in Switzerland eating a hearty goulash soup. You'll see that it was worth it."

"Really?" Bruno looked up at him with the trusting expression of a toddler.

"If I say so."

Eventually, Bruno nodded. "Alright, I'll try." Leaning heavily on Felix, he got to his feet. He was trembling all over, but he was standing.

Nervously, Felix looked around in all directions. Just then, Bärbel appeared at the top of the ridge, signaling everything was fine with them. With that burden sliding from his shoulders, he stood more upright. In response, he gave her a thumbs-up.

Then began the agonizing slow ascent. Felix climbed ahead, creating extra secure steps in the snow. Bruno followed close behind. Despite their snail's pace, Bruno's breathing was jerky and irregular. They had barely climbed five meters when shouts from below reached their ears.

Felix's mind raced. It had to be a border patrol, or the

mountain rescue—which ultimately amounted to the same. He risked a sidelong glance at Bruno, who stood petrified next to him, his face a mask of horror.

For a moment, he toyed with the idea of giving Bruno a push so he would tumble down the slope. Felix could use the diversion to sprint up the mountain to save himself and warn the women.

That would be the logical decision. Bruno was lost anyway. In the same second, he discarded the notion; he wouldn't sacrifice another person to save himself.

CHAPTER 17

Bärbel had watched Bruno's fall in shocked awe until, after what seemed like an eternity, he stopped and remained motionless. She was itching to climb down to provide first aid, but she respected Felix's decision that she and Astrid should climb to the ridge and wait there.

One gaze at Astrid's chalk-white face confirmed this decision. A break in the sun would do her good.

"Come on, let's climb up," she said gently.

Astrid nodded with wide eyes. "Do you think he's dead?"

"Certainly not. That kind of slide looks much more dangerous than it actually is." Bärbel put all her confidence into her voice. "As soon as Felix reaches him, we'll know more. But first, we need to get out of the danger zone."

"Will we be buried by an avalanche otherwise?"

"No." Bärbel shook her head. The possibility always existed, but the current risk of an avalanche was very low. The more realistic threat was that someone had heard the screams and was looking for them. She had no illusions about where the mountain rescue team's loyalty would lie, if they weren't found by a border patrol first.

Bärbel took the lead. Breaking trail in the sticky snow was hard work. After just a few minutes, sweat was running down her back as she fought her way upward step by step. She recognized with admiration Felix's incredible endurance, even though he was at least twice her age.

Every few steps, she turned to check on Astrid, whose face had frozen into a pained grimace. At least she was keeping up without complaint; the injured knee seemed to be causing her surprisingly little trouble.

After about fifteen minutes, they reached the ridge.

"Look, how beautiful!" Bärbel exclaimed. Before them stretched a fairytale winter landscape. In the distance, the majestic peaks of the Gämpiflua and Sulzfluh rose into the brilliant blue sky.

She glanced down the slope, where she could make out Felix next to Bruno, neither of them moving. Shivers ran up and down her spine. Should she call out? Even at the risk someone else might hear?

At that exact moment, Felix turned his head. Relieved, she signaled to him everything was fine with them. In response, he gave a thumbs up. Relieved, she turned to Astrid. "Felix and Bruno are doing fine."

"Thank God." Astrid was very pale around the nose.

To cheer her up, Bärbel pointed toward a peak. "Do you see that mountain top over there? That is in Switzerland."

"It's still so far?" Astrid replied meekly.

"Don't worry," Bärbel reassured her. "The border is much closer, about halfway between here and the peak." She wasn't sure exactly where the border crossing was, since she had never been up here before.

"Come on, let's find a comfortable spot to sit down." Bärbel walked a few steps until she found the perfect resting place: a flat stone behind the rock face that shielded them both from the wind and from unwanted glances. On the south side it was pleasantly warm—exactly as Felix had predicted.

Bärbel stretched out her legs and was about to lean against the warm rock face when she noticed that Astrid was shivering violently. Concerned, she asked, "Are you cold?"

"N... n... no." Astrid's teeth were chattering so hard she couldn't form a coherent word.

Bärbel recognized the symptoms: traumatic shock. In medical school, they had learned that sugar could help in such situations. So she rummaged through her backpack. They had eaten most of the provisions, but at the very bottom she found a wrapped jam sandwich.

"Here," she said, handing it to Astrid. "This will help you."

"I can't possibly accept that," Astrid protested.

"You need it more than I do." Bärbel smiled at her. "Come on, eat so you can get your strength back."

Casting a grateful look, Astrid accepted the bread and bit into it. Time passed painfully slowly; no sound reached them from below. Shouldn't the two men be on their way up by now? Bärbel struggled with herself until she couldn't stand it any longer. She crawled to the edge of the rock to look down the other side. As soon as she left the sheltered spot, a sharp wind blew around her nose. Shivering, she squinted against the blinding brightness until she spotted Felix and Bruno, who seemed to still be in the same place. *What are they doing down there so long?*

She was tempted to climb down to provide first aid if necessary, but Felix had indicated everything was fine—and had unambiguously ordered her to wait up here with Astrid. Her gaze swept further down the valley and her heart skipped a beat: two dark dots stood out against the snow. Once more she squinted until there was no doubt the dots were moving.

Hopefully those weren't soldiers on patrol, searching the region for illegal border crossers. She retreated behind the protective rock outcropping, where Astrid was leaning exhausted against the rock face, her face turned to the sun, eyes closed.

"How are you feeling?" Bärbel asked.

"Better," Astrid murmured without opening her eyes. "My knee hardly hurts anymore."

"Would you like something to drink?" When Astrid nodded, Bärbel handed her the water bottle.

"There's hardly anything left."

"That's not a problem. I'll make more." Astrid handed back the empty bottle, and Bärbel stuffed clean snow into the wide neck, before placing the bottle in the sun so it would melt into drinking water.

Astrid watched with interest until she suddenly asked, "Do you think Bruno is dead?"

"No," Bärbel assured her. "Felix gave me a sign that everything's fine. We just have to wait until they reach us." Secretly, she had doubts about whether Bruno would manage the climb. She prepared herself for a long wait, since it would definitely take some time. The uncertainty of who or what those two black dots were nagged at her, too. She sent a quick prayer up to heaven that their group of four wouldn't be discovered. Since she didn't want to frighten Astrid even more, she kept her concerns to herself.

"What happens if Bruno can't make the climb?" Astrid persisted.

Bärbel hesitated. After asking herself the same question, she hadn't found a satisfactory answer. She would have preferred not to say anything, but Astrid's pleading look wouldn't let up. "If it comes to that, Felix will let us know what to do."

"How will he do that?" Astrid started to tremble again.

"Either he'll climb up, or I'll go down."

"I'm not going down there again. The climb up was bad enough."

"You don't have to," Bärbel reassured her. "If it's even necessary, I'll go alone. You can wait here."

"Without you?" Astrid shook her head vehemently. "I can't do that. What would I do if neither one of you comes back?"

"Don't worry. Nothing has happened yet. We'll sit here and wait until we hear from Felix." Astrid seemed to be overwhelmed by her fear, therefore Bärbel considered her options to distract the other woman. "Do you have family?"

A wistful expression settled on Astrid's face. "I do. My parents and two younger brothers. Until recently, we lived together in Frankfurt. You know, my mother is Aryan; because of her we were somewhat protected."

"Why did you flee? Alone?"

Astrid grimaced. "I covered up the star while walking on the street. Someone apparently reported me to the Gestapo."

"Is that so serious?" Bärbel couldn't imagine someone running away because of such a trivial matter.

"You have no idea! As a Jew, you have no rights, even the smallest offense can be punished by death." Anger at the injustice brought color to Astrid's cheeks.

"The Gestapo imposes the death penalty because someone doesn't wear the yellow star?" That was harsh even for the Nazis.

"Not directly. But if you're caught out without wearing the star or even just covering it, for example by holding a purse in front of your chest, you'll be arrested." Astrid's voice had a bitter undertone. "It's up to the officer's discretion what happens next. Some may let you go with a warning, while others use the opportunity to send you to a concentration camp, where you're either immediately shot, allegedly 'while trying to escape,' or succumb to the horrific living conditions within a few weeks."

Bärbel shook her head in disbelief. "I had no idea."

"Most people don't, as long as they're not directly affected. The Nazis are very skilled at concealing the worst atrocities. Even Aryan friends of ours, whom Mother visits regularly, consider her accounts to be grossly exaggerated."

"So you fled?"

"I feel so shabby."

"But why?"

"Because I abandoned my family. Without my wages and food ration cards, it will be even worse for them. We barely had enough to eat as it was."

This was also news to Bärbel. She knew that Jews were prohibited from buying certain foods declared as scarce commodities, but the notion that they had to starve seemed far-fetched. Apparently the Nazis had been very successful with their cover-up strategy if even Bärbel, who considered herself part of the resistance, knew little to nothing about the many hardships her Jewish compatriots faced.

Ashamed, she said, "Your family surely wants you to be safe."

Suddenly tears ran down Astrid's face. "Of course they do, but I still feel so shabby. Mother even gave me her gold wedding ring to pay the guide."

Bärbel put a comforting arm around Astrid's shoulders and let her cry. Sometimes tears were the best medicine. As she looked at Astrid, she was reminded of her own situation. Now she realized why Felix had said her silver necklace wouldn't be enough. The price of freedom was high.

She tried to chase away the gloomy thoughts and quickly put on a confident expression, but Astrid had noticed her distress and asked, "What's bothering you?"

"Nothing."

"I can see something's wrong."

Bärbel gave a deep sigh. "I don't have any money to bribe the border guards, just my silver necklace. Felix said it probably wouldn't be enough."

Astrid fell silent for a while before saying, "I still have my mother's ring. You can have it."

"I absolutely cannot accept that," Bärbel protested.

"Of course you can. I didn't have to pay Felix because I took the place of another woman who didn't make it to the meeting point. Bruno suspects she was arrested." She grabbed Bärbel's hand. "You've taken such good care of me. Let me help you. Please!"

Reluctantly, Bärbel nodded. "Agreed. But only as an absolute last resort. First we'll try with my necklace."

The next moment loud shouts reached them from below.

"Wait here," Bärbel whispered and crawled to the edge of the rock. Felix and Bruno were on their feet. When Felix noticed her, he gestured for her to hide.

Regardless, she risked another peek around the corner. The two black dots she had seen earlier had come close enough for her to identify them as uniformed figures—a third had joined the first two—heading directly toward Bruno and Felix.

With a pounding heart, she crawled backward, frantically weighing her options. Should she and Astrid make a run for it, trying to reach the border on their own?

No, the undertaking was too risky. Bärbel shook her head. She didn't even know exactly where the green—or currently white—border lay, and she knew even less how the guards would react if two refugees showed up without a guide.

For now, they were safe. If necessary, they could squeeze between the rock outcropping and the snow wall to avoid being seen. With swift movements, she began to erase their footprints in the snow. Every trace of their presence had to disappear. Soon sweat beaded on her forehead.

"What's happening down there?" Astrid whispered.

"Felix and Bruno have been discovered. Three men are approaching them," Bärbel replied, concealing that the strangers were in uniform.

"What are we supposed to do?" Astrid's lips were trembling.

"First of all: stay calm. We'll hide and wait." She motioned for Astrid to follow her. Her backpack strapped to her front, she crawled on all fours into the hollow space between the snow wall and the rock. When she had gone far enough not to be seen from outside, she turned and leaned against the warm stone with her knees pulled up, the backpack beside her.

The melting snow dripped uncomfortably down Bärbel's collar, so she changed her position until she finally found a dry spot. Next to her, Astrid was shaking like an aspen leaf.

Bärbel feared she hadn't fully recovered from the shock. In this condition, Astrid's behavior was unpredictable, which might become dangerous. So she took her hand and whispered, "They can't see us in here."

"What happens if they search for us?"

"Why would they do that? Nobody knows the group consists of four people and not just two."

"They'll see our tracks."

Fear squeezed the breath from Bärbel's lungs. Somehow she managed to reply in a calm voice, "Those could be the men's footprints. Felix will surely come up with a believable story, if the strangers aren't just harmless hikers anyway."

"You think it's not the border police?"

Bärbel chose not to answer. "As long as we sit here quiet as mice, they won't find us."

For a while it was silent, then Astrid whispered, "I'm scared."

"Think of something nice," Bärbel suggested, rubbing circles on the back of Astrid's hand with her thumb to instill confidence in her.

If the patrol did indeed pass their hiding place, they mustn't make a single sound. Bärbel already regretted having crawled first into the crevice, because in this position she could hardly prevent Astrid from running away, straight into the arms of the patrol, in case she panicked.

CHAPTER 18

They stood completely exposed on the slope, like shooting targets at a fairground. Even the flat rock that had ended Bruno's slide offered no cover whatsoever.

Felix grabbed Bruno's arm and dragged him diagonally across the slope. His target was the rocky outcrop at the edge, though he knew deep in his heart how futile the attempt was, since their footprints in the fresh snow would be clearly visible to their pursuers.

He racked his brain for a way out. They could comply with the order and surrender to the police. At least Felix could hope for mercy if he sweet-talked Fritz enough—the same though didn't apply to Bruno, who would inevitably be swinging from the gallows in the marketplace shortly. Center of another gruesome spectacle to intimidate the villagers.

He increased his pace, mercilessly pulling the stumbling Bruno behind him. If he wanted to be able to look at himself in the mirror again, he couldn't hand over a man whose only crime was being Jewish.

As long as there was even the faintest chance, he would

fight. A quick glance back told him the three pursuers were gaining ground. They had approached close enough for him to identify their dark uniforms as border patrol.

"Stop! Hands up!" The barking command tore through the mountain air like the crack of a whip.

His thoughts raced, his heart pounding brutally against his ribs. Unforgivingly, he tugged at Bruno's arm. If they could make it over the flat rocky outcrop... the stones would provide cover. Protected from view and without leaving footprints on the hard surface, they had a chance to mislead their pursuers.

In the next moment, a shot cracked through the silence. Instinctively, Felix threw himself into the snow. Bruno though seemed frozen to a stone statue, his dark silhouette standing out against the brilliant blue sky.

"Get down!" hissed Felix. "On the ground!"

Bruno didn't budge. He seemed completely unaware of what was happening around him.

His heart pounding, Felix crawled toward him. He ignored the wet snow falling into his collar and the numbing cold in his bare fingers.

"Hit the ground!" he snapped at Bruno a second time. At the same time he stretched out both hands, grabbed Bruno's calves and yanked sharply, just as a second shot pierced the air. The echo reverberated off the mountains sounding like cruel mocking laughter.

Before Felix's eyes, Bruno staggered, his face a mask of disbelieving horror. Seconds later he dropped like a felled tree. Felix's hope that he had brought him down by pulling his legs vanished as soon as Bruno hit the ground.

Blood poured from his throat. It formed an ugly dark stain on his jacket and seeped into the untouched snow, leaving bright red spots on the perfect white.

The gruesome sight told Felix it was over. Regardless, he

crawled to Bruno's head, where blood gurgled from his shot-through throat, a terrible, wet sound Felix would never forget for the rest of his life.

The wide-open eyes became glassy. Felix couldn't do more than kneel next to the dying man, placing a hand on his cheek and pressing firmly. A final moment of connection rumbled between them before the life escaped Bruno's body with a last rasping breath. The man he had meant to lead to freedom had died in his arms.

His blood transformed the snow into a gruesome pattern of red and white. But Felix didn't have time to mourn. He had to save his own life. Crunching footsteps revealed that the border guards had resumed their pursuit. A mixture of horror, grief and hot fury rushed through Felix's veins.

These filthy Nazi pigs had extinguished another life, killed another human being just because he wanted to escape their cruelty. If Felix didn't want to become their next victim, it was high time for him to disappear. Casting a glance toward the ridge, he made sure Bärbel had followed his orders and taken herself and Astrid to safety. However, their hiding place wouldn't remain undiscovered for long if the border guards searched the slope.

Felix fought against the rising nausea, swallowed it along with his scruples, and kicked hard against Bruno's shoulder. The corpse began to slide, slowly at first, then faster and faster, following the same track he had left during his fateful fall less than an hour ago. Past the bare rock, which had stopped him the first time, further and further, all the way to the end of the slope.

Felix's stomach rebelled at this last undignified service to his dead charge as he whispered, "Please forgive me."

The border guards reacted as he'd envisioned, changing their direction. Felix lay flat in the snow and observed their movements like a predator in ambush. Just as he was about to breathe a sigh of relief, the small group split up: Two men hurried down to Bruno's corpse, while the third raised his rifle and headed directly toward Felix.

In a fight with the armed border guard, he would come out on the losing end. His only advantage was decades of mountain experience. So he sought salvation in flight, scrambled to his feet and hastened across the slope toward the rocky outcrop, behind which a steep drop was hidden.

The guard recognized his intention as harsh commands immediately cut through the air: "Stop! *Stehen bleiben!*"

Felix ignored them; from the stature and voice, he knew his pursuer to be the party-loyal Oberführer Schmitt. Schmitt was one of the few policemen who had internalized the Nazi ideology; even generous bribes wouldn't convince him to turn a blind eye. Especially not when it came to exterminating Jews or holding accountable those who helped these unwanted compatriots.

Instead of stopping, Felix accelerated his steps. His mouth wide open, he ran gasping through the slushy snow, resisting the urge to look back. Stitches in his side turned every step into agony as he focused on a single goal: getting himself over the rocky outcrop.

He was just a few steps away when a bullet whizzed past his ear in a sharp whistle. Snow splashed where the projectile struck. The booming crack echoed from the mountains multiple times. Following a sudden inspiration, Felix roared like a wounded animal and let himself roll to the side as if the bullet had hit him.

The rocky ledge was within reach. Out of the corner of his eye, he noticed Schmitt lowering his rifle. That was exactly the reaction he had hoped for. In an explosive movement, Felix jumped up and threw himself over the rocky ledge in a desperate dive. He silently prayed there would be enough snow on the other side to cushion his fall.

The seconds in the air stretched endlessly followed by a brutal landing. A sharp stone bored deep into his hip, the impact forcing the air from his lungs. Black dots danced before his eyes.

Summoning all his willpower, he focused on the next steps: In spite of his trembling hands, he tore his backpack off in a quick movement and shoved it forcefully down the slope. The scraping sound thundered in his ears. Felix wasted no time watching the sliding gear, but turned in the opposite direction. The backpack would create a false trail that would buy him precious time.

His injured hip protested loudly as he took a detour up through the snow, using his reverse-nailed soles to leave tracks leading down toward the backpack, before stepping onto rocky ground where his footprints weren't visible.

He estimated having a three-minute head start, before Schmitt reached the outcrop. Three miserable minutes to climb high enough to hide himself in the rugged rock formation above.

At every step, his injured hip sent a stabbing pain all the way down to his toes. He gritted his teeth and marched on. His gasping breath formed clouds in the icy air, but giving up was not an option. Not only his life depended on getting to the ridge, but also that of the two women hiding there. He couldn't let them down. Not after everything that already happened.

The mountains had taught him that often pure will made the difference between life and death. And he intended to live. He and the two women. On this hellish journey, he swore to himself, he would not lose a second person.

Sweat ran into his eyes, burning like fire; however, Felix had no hand free to wipe his forehead. The desperation of a hunted man propelled him forward, as he climbed the steep slope using hands and feet, pulling himself up on rock ledges that would have been insurmountable under normal circumstances. His muscles screamed and every single cell in his body protested against the extreme exertion.

He ignored the pain shooting through him in waves. A single thought drove him on: escaping the border guards. Just as he was pulling himself up on an exposed ledge, he glanced from the corner of his eye to see his pursuer climbing over the rocky outcrop. Adrenaline pumped through his veins and gave him the bear-like strength he needed to push himself up.

Completely exhausted, he rolled over the edge and pressed himself flat against the stone. Exercising superhuman effort, he suppressed his panting as he observed through a narrow gap how Oberführer Schmitt looked around in all directions.

Once Schmitt discovered Felix's discarded backpack several meters down the slope, he called out, "Got you! Now you won't get away from me!"

Relief heightened Felix's spirits, because the false trail had done its job. By the time Schmitt discovered his mistake, Felix would be literally over the hills and far away. The next second, though, a cold shiver ran down his back. Stock-still, he pressed himself deeper into the ground as if he could merge with the stone and become invisible. Schmitt had turned around and discovered Felix's footprints, which led through the deep snow straight to the rock formation behind which he was hiding.

The crunch of Schmitt's steps drowned out even the rushing of Felix's own blood in his ears. If the border guard found footprints on the stone, Felix would be done for. Schmitt came closer, knelt down, examined the imprint in the snow and slowly shook his head. He stood up again, turned around and descended the slope after the fallen backpack.

Felix slowly exhaled. As he inhaled once more, relief flowed through him like a warm balm. Once again, the reverse-nailed soles had saved his life. In his mind, he thanked his father who had taught him the smuggler's trick. However, he wasn't out of trouble yet. His nerves taut as a bowstring, he racked his brain about how to leave his makeshift hiding place without being seen.

He pricked his ears to catch the slightest sound. The silence in the mountains was deceptive; every crackle, every rolling stone, every step carried far. So he waited and counted to twenty until he was absolutely certain that Oberführer Schmitt was no longer going to look upward. Then he peeled himself off the ground, slowly and carefully like a predator stalking its prey.

On nimble feet he climbed toward the ridge under the protection of the rocks. He used every unevenness, every projection to pull himself higher. The exertion made sweat flow in streams down his back. He wished he were twenty again; back then, an ordeal like this one hadn't bothered him —on the contrary, he had welcomed the challenge. Felix encouraged himself: He might no longer have the strength and stamina of a youth, but he could trump that with decades of mountain experience.

Undeterred, he kept climbing, although the rocky ground scraped his hands bloody and sharp stone splinters dug into his skin. The pain was secondary, and would be forgotten by the next day. In the here and now, fear for his very life drove him. The higher he climbed, the stronger the wind blew, lashing snow into his face, biting into his skin. It didn't stop him from continuing to scramble, his gaze fixed firmly on the ridge.

The trickiest section lay ahead, because he had to return to the broad slope to reach the spot where Astrid and Bärbel were waiting for him.

A gnawing unease tugged at him. How had the two women fared? He fervently hoped they hadn't witnessed

Bruno's death. Even he, who considered himself hardened, gagged at the memory of the snow stained red with blood. He had to banish the gruesome images from his head. During the next part of their escape, he needed a clear mind.

Nothing on this tour had gone as it should. Only if he kept his wits about him would he be able to bring the matter to a good end and save himself and the two women.

Reaching the top, he ducked behind a rocky outcrop and peered down. The two border guards had placed Bruno's body on a makeshift stretcher, and were now dragging him across the slope. The strange procession moved toward the third man, who had apparently found the backpack and was waiting for them next to it.

Felix watched them until they disappeared behind a rock formation. As soon as they were out of sight, he exploded into a burst of strength attacking the last few meters to the ridge and immediately threw himself behind the outcrop, where he hoped to find Astrid and Bärbel.

Gasping, he struggled for breath. They weren't safe yet, but they had gained time. Precious time that had increased their chances of escaping unharmed.

CHAPTER 19

Two bangs shattered the silence and echoed in Astrid's ears. She wanted to jump up to investigate, yet Bärbel's firm grip on her arm held her back.

"Stay here! We mustn't show ourselves," Bärbel hissed.

"Those were gunshots!" The growing panic pushed aside all caution. "If Bruno or Felix were hit, they need our help. We have to get to them right now."

Bärbel sighed. "We can't help them. We'll only achieve one thing—letting the border guards know we're here so they can hunt us too."

Paralyzed, Astrid sank to the ground, staring at the wall of snow directly in front of them. Suddenly, the white element seemed threatening, even hostile. She chewed on her fingernails while waiting to see what would happen. In her mind, she heard the shots over and over again, followed by the shouting, and she imagined the bloodiest scene until she finally couldn't stand it anymore. "How long are we going to sit around here doing nothing?"

Bärbel shrugged. "I can't tell you that. In any case, it's much too early to check on them."

"How can you sit here so calmly when..." Astrid's voice broke.

"It's hard, but you must stay calm. Right now, we can't help anyone but ourselves."

Silence spread between them, the minutes stretching into an agonizing eternity. About a thousand times, Astrid was on the verge of jumping up and crawling out of their hiding place. Each time, only fear of the border guards—and Bärbel's hand on her arm—held her back.

Eventually, the crunch of boots in the snow reached her ear, followed by heavy panting. As the noises approached, her muscles tensed.

"Bärbel," she whispered, her voice barely more than a breath, "someone's coming!"

Bärbel seemed to have heard it too, because she put her finger to her lips and pulled Astrid deeper into the narrow space between snow and rock. Astrid pressed herself against the rough surface of the stone, digging her fingers into Bärbel's hand. At least she wasn't left alone to her fate.

Moments later the entrance to their hideout darkened. Astrid rammed the ball of her thumb between her teeth to keep from screaming out loud. A figure stood directly in front of the entrance, blocking the sun and plunging the hiding place into a dusky twilight. Astrid squeezed her eyes shut. Her pulse pounded so loudly in her ears she feared the intruder might hear it.

Endless seconds she sat frozen in the semi-darkness, hoping the person would move on, wouldn't discover them. She sent a desperate prayer to heaven, begging to be spared, to be allowed to survive just this one time.

"It's me, Felix," whispered a familiar voice.

Astrid opened her eyes. The tension slowly drained from her limbs as she released a breath.

Bärbel, crouching beside her, recovered quicker and answered: "Thank God! You're back."

"What happened to Bruno?" Astrid could barely croak out the words.

"Let me get in first," Felix replied, squeezing into the narrow gap. "He didn't make it. He's dead. Shot by the police."

A sob escaped Astrid's throat. Tears she had held back for hours ran hot down her face. Images of Bruno, nervous and uncertain as he trudged through the snow, and Felix repeatedly encouraging him, appeared before her eyes. Now he was dead, shot by the border guards while she had hidden, just a few meters away. Gnawing guilt ate into her heart. She should have prevented his death.

Bärbel placed a comforting hand on her arm. "Maybe it's better this way."

"How can you say such a thing?" Astrid glared at her, shocked by the cold-hearted reply.

"If they had caught him alive, they would certainly torture him until he betrayed his helpers."

"What cruel comfort," Astrid whispered, feeling like she might faint at any moment.

"The only comfort we have." Bärbel didn't seem particularly affected by the situation.

Felix intervened. "I don't think they're following us. But if they are, this hiding place isn't safe enough. We need to move on quickly."

Horror keeping her in a severe grip, Astrid listened to the heartless conversation between the two. How could they worry about their own safety at a time like this, instead of mourning poor Bruno? Disturbed, she turned away. Were these the people she was entrusting her life to? The people who were supposed to help her flee to freedom?

"You can't do this!" she cried.

Bärbel placed her hands on Astrid's shoulders in an almost painful grip. "Look at me."

Astrid obeyed with reluctance, catching Bärbel giving Felix a meaningful look before he took a step back.

"Bruno is dead. We can't help him anymore. But we can help ourselves. Or do you want to end up like him?"

Unable to respond, she rocked her head back and forth. Bruno was dead. Shot in the back. Murdered in cold blood. No, she didn't want to end up like him. She shook her head.

"Are you able to get up?"

Astrid swallowed hard. Fog swirled through her brain, preventing a clear thought. Finally, she stammered: "I... I don't know."

"Your mother would want you to arrive safely in Switzerland." Bärbel's voice was insistent. "Don't you think her sacrifice shouldn't be in vain?"

The unspoken meaning of her words hung heavily in the air: the golden wedding ring her mother had given to buy Astrid's freedom. Gradually the fog in her brain cleared. The words penetrated, awakening something in her she feared she had lost: the absolute will to survive, the hope for a future. Slowly she nodded. "Yes, Mother wants me to be safe," she whispered, "and Father too."

"Certainly your brothers as well," Bärbel added.

The thought of her two brothers, always ready for mischief, brought a fleeting smile to Astrid's face. In their childhood, they had been in a constant, loving competition, bickering incessantly without diminishing their deep affection for one another. In times of need, each of the three was ready to do anything for the others.

Her brothers would tease her for the rest of her life if she gave up now. She didn't want to grant them that triumph. On the contrary, she would send them a postcard from

Switzerland delivering the proud note: "I made it!" She lifted her chin, relishing the renewed energy flowing through her veins. "Yes, I can do this."

"Then let's go." Giving a grim nod, Bärbel shouldered her backpack.

Astrid reached for hers, but Felix beat her to it. "Let me take it. We'll be faster that way."

He grabbed her backpack with one hand, while taking hold of her forearm with the other one. His firm, warm grip ignited a spark of hope in her heart against all reason. Perhaps all was not lost yet.

As long as Felix was with them, they had a chance. Then her thoughts drifted back to Bruno. The memory hit her like a thunderbolt; her hope burst like a soap bubble. He, too, had trusted Felix. And now he was dead.

Out of the blue, tears ran down Astrid's cheeks. She no longer wanted to flee, she didn't want to postpone the inevitable. If she had to die anyway, she wanted to do it on her own terms. She wished to remain sitting in her hiding place for all eternity. If only she could turn to stone—then the Nazis couldn't harm her anymore.

Felix seemed not to notice her emotional chaos and continued the gentle pull on her hand. Thus she had no choice but to crawl out of the hiding place. Once outside, he helped her to her feet. She turned her head, taking particular care not to gaze down the slope, where in her mind's eye she could see Bruno lying.

Dead.

Murdered.

A voice in her head whispered: "Bärbel is right. You can't do anything for him. For his sake, you must continue. He paid the money for the passage. He would want at least one of you to make it to freedom."

Next to her stood Bärbel, eyeing Felix. "Where's your backpack?"

"I pushed it down the slope," he answered. "The border guards should think it was me. It will take them a while to figure out that I actually went uphill, which will give us a head start." He glanced over his shoulder, as if expecting pursuers at any moment. "We have to get going. I know a shelter where we can hide."

"Don't the police know about the shelter?" asked Bärbel skeptically.

A mocking smile played around Felix's lips, the first since Bruno's death. "They know the hut, but not the secret hiding place beneath the wooden floor. We can wait there if they come looking for us."

Astrid shuddered. She preferred not to imagine how cramped and oppressive this underground hideout would be.

Felix turned into business mode as he ordered: "I'll walk in first place, Astrid in the middle, Bärbel takes up the rear. We have no time to lose, so I'll keep the pace high."

"I'll walk until I drop dead," Astrid assured him with more conviction than she felt. She counted on the fear of becoming the laughingstock of her brothers to evoke bear-like strength in her limbs.

Felix patted her on the shoulder. "You'd make a good smuggler—you've got grit."

Flattered, Astrid fell in step between him and Bärbel as they set off. Felix hadn't lied: his pace was murderous. After a few minutes, she was gasping with her mouth hanging wide open, her heart hammering in staccato against her ribs to pump oxygen into her screaming muscles. Sweat ran down her back in rivulets until her undershirt clung damp, disgusting and cold to her skin. At least her tortured toes in the too small shoes eventually went numb.

The one thing which troubled her, was the fact they were

steadily moving away from the peak in Switzerland Bärbel had pointed to earlier. She didn't get a chance to ask Felix about it, since he drove them mercilessly over bumpy mountain paths, through valley depressions and over snow-covered knolls. On the south side of the mountain, there was hardly any snow left, so he didn't bother making footsteps for her to step into.

At some point, Astrid stopped noticing the magnificent landscape around her. She stared directly downward to the spot where she wanted to place her next step. Whenever she couldn't see Felix's brown hiking boots anymore, she lifted her head, fixed her gaze on his back and made a double effort to close the gap.

As they passed a small snow patch, she reached down, wiped her face with the cool mass and stuffed the rest into her mouth. Greedily she swallowed the melted drops to soothe her thirsty throat.

She had completely lost track of time—orientation long before—when at some point her bad knee began to throb. Every step shot a stabbing pain up her entire leg. Clenching her teeth, she marched on. Giving up was not an option. Meter by meter she fought her way forward until she began to hallucinate. One second, Bruno was marching beside her, very much alive; in the next, he lay dying on the ground, his reproachful look cutting her to the bone.

A minute later, her brothers walked next to her, incessantly teasing her for being too slow, just to reach out a helping hand the next moment. Once again she lost sight of Felix's boots and raised her head. Straight ahead the sun hung blood-red over a peak.

Blinded, she looked aside, where a mirage floated in the air: in a depression stood a wooden hut, nestled against a slope. She blinked several times, but the image remained intact.

The hut was real. In her chest hope rose that this forced march would eventually come to an end. Conjuring up the last remnant of her energy, Astrid quickened her steps. Once they came close enough, she saw a thin plume of smoke rising from the chimney like a curling ghost.

Astrid stopped so abruptly that Bärbel bumped into her and asked: "What's wrong?"

"Someone's there." Astrid pointed to the plume of smoke.

"That is the old shepherd, he lives in the hut," Felix explained.

"I thought the sheep are driven down from the alpine pastures in September and stay over winter in the valley." Bärbel seemed knowledgeable.

"That's right." Felix rubbed his chin. "A few years ago, the old shepherd decided to leave the herding of the sheep to his son-in-law. Since then, he stays up here year-round. He doesn't agree with the Nazis."

Astrid got the impression Felix was telling only part of the truth. As long as the shepherd didn't betray them to the border police, she didn't care. She yearned to finally, finally, take off the painfully tight shoes and put her feet up. Another thought struck her like lightning: "Do you think there might be another person in the hut? The border guards could have gotten there before us."

"Unlikely, but possible." Felix chewed on his lower lip until he pointed to a pile of stones. "You two hide there, while I'll go and check."

Before Astrid could ask what they should do if border police were actually waiting in the hut, he had marched off.

"Come with me." Bärbel walked the few steps toward the pile of stones. Astrid had no choice but to follow her. Waiting in their hiding place, the smell of wood smoke reached her nose—conjuring images of a cozy room with an open fireplace. How she longed for a cup of hot coffee.

After a seemingly endless wait, which in reality probably lasted just a few minutes, Felix stepped out of the hut again, waving at them. "You can come, all clear."

Astrid's exhausted legs mustered a final effort. The moment she crossed the threshold, her entire strength seeped out of her. Her knees gave way, and she sank onto the roughly hewn shoe rack standing in the entrance.

CHAPTER 20

Felix covered the last few meters to the cabin alone. He made sure the women had disappeared behind the pile of stones before he raised his hand to knock on the door.

It took a while until footsteps sounded, and the door opened with a creak. The old shepherd stood before him, leaning on a gnarled staff. He had hardly changed over the years. A long white beard reached almost to his chest. The light blue eyes in his wrinkled face were watchful.

As soon as he recognized Felix, his expression brightened. "Felix, how wonderful to see you. I so rarely have visitors." He stepped aside with an inviting gesture. "What have you brought me this time?"

Felix shrugged awkwardly. It was the first time he'd visited Guido empty-handed. "I need your help. Two women are waiting outside. The border patrol is after us. I had to drop my backpack along the way to lay a false trail."

The old man nodded. For almost ten years, he had been resisting the Nazis by offering shelter to smugglers, black marketers, and fugitives; after all this time, nothing seemed to surprise him anymore. "Bring them in. We'll prepare the hiding place just in case."

For the first time on this horrific day, Felix actually believed things might turn out alright. They were safe with Guido. The old man was reliable and the secret hiding place under the wooden floor had been searched for, yet never been found by many law enforcement officers over the decades.

As the women stepped inside the cabin, he swept his gaze across the landscape one more time. Nobody was in sight. He exhaled a sigh of relief and instructed the women: "Put on some dry clothes and sit by the stove." The cabin consisted of a single large room, the roaring stove serving for both heating and cooking, while Guido's sleeping area was separated from the rest of the room by a folding screen.

Behind it lay the hiding place and the entrance to the ancient tunnel that ended next to the outhouse, about fifty meters from the cabin. Felix himself had never used the tunnel—he knew about it through his father's and grandfather's stories.

No sooner had Astrid sunk onto a wooden chair than her eyes closed. The day's events and the forced march of the last few hours were taking their toll on her. Bärbel, though, kept herself upright, despite the visible exhaustion on her face.

"Give me a hand," Guido said to Felix, leading him to the sleeping area behind the folding screen. Together they pushed aside the heavy wooden chest. The old piece scraped across the floor until it revealed the trapdoor underneath.

"Is it the same mechanism as in the living room?" Felix asked. Under the table was a second secret room where Guido stored his provisions—this one well-known to the police, who believed it to be the only secret room in the cabin.

"Yes."

"Can you manage to push the chest back by yourself?"

Felix studied the old man. He was well over eighty, thin, with sinewy limbs.

"We'll take the heavy things out, then it should work."

"Thank you for helping us." Aiding their escape posed dangers for Guido too. Depending on which border guard might show up, even an old man couldn't count on leniency.

Guido shrugged. "I'm old. They can't do anything to me that I'm not already prepared for."

Bärbel's voice wafted over from the main room, "Can I help with something?"

"No need." Guido stood up with difficulty, rubbed his hip, and walked to her. "If you want to make yourself useful, please put on some water for coffee."

While Bärbel busied herself at the cast-iron stove, Felix lifted the trapdoor and inspected the hiding place in the dim light. Just as he was about to climb down, Guido handed him an oil lamp.

"Take this. You'll need it. No one's been down there for a while. Check what you'll need, besides fresh water and some blankets."

Felix jumped into the hip-high space, inhaled the smell of moldy wood and damp earth before turning around to take the lamp. The soil was supported by wooden beams much like inside a mine. A bench stood against the approximately two-meter-long wall, and an empty shelf was fastened on the short side.

However, he was more interested in the entrance to the secret tunnel, which he couldn't find.

Guido seemed to guess what he was looking for. His voice hovered from above, "Behind the wooden bench. It's less than eighty centimeters high. The exit of the tunnel is next to the outhouse, not visible from the house."

"I hope we won't need to use it."

"Your father said the same thing." Back then, Guido's

father had been the shepherd, and Felix's father had sought shelter with him after an adventurous journey.

"Apart from a shot in the thigh, he made it off the mountain in one piece. Afterward, he had to lay low for several years—those were lean times for us."

"Once you've figured out what you need, come back up. We still have plenty of things to prepare."

As Bärbel brewed coffee and set the table, the two men moved the guests' belongings into the hiding place—except for the wet socks and shoes drying in front of the stove. Everyone would have to grab theirs, if the border police knocked on the door and they had to disappear. They equipped the hideout with a carafe of water, provisions, blankets, and a chamber pot. In case they needed to move quickly, they left the trapdoor lid open.

"Food is ready," Bärbel called.

Felix cast a final gaze around the hideout, making sure everything was prepared for an emergency, until a scary notion caused him to shiver. "How do we get out of the hiding place if they take you away for questioning?"

"They've never done that before," Guido grumbled. "If anything goes wrong, you'll have to escape through the tunnel."

"Are you sure it's still passable?"

"More like crawlable." Guido rubbed his chin. "I should think so."

An uneasy feeling crept into Felix's bones. He reassured himself it was just a precaution, and they'd never have to test whether the tunnel would actually hold.

Bärbel woke Astrid, who joined them at the table, her eyelids drooping. Just now Felix realized how hungry he was. The day's exertions hadn't left him unscathed, and he hoped the journey would hold no more nasty surprises.

Tonight they would sleep at Guido's, the next day they

urgently needed to reach the border. The guards worked in a rotation system to prevent the establishment of routines. Tomorrow was the last day the two bribed border guards, Meinhold and Christoph, would be on duty at St. Antönier Joch; afterward, they would be transferred to another border crossing for several weeks. Unfortunately, Felix didn't know where that would be. Moreover, he had no idea who would replace them. Therefore, tomorrow was Astrid and Bärbel's last chance to flee to Switzerland for at least several weeks.

"Why are you helping us, Guido?" Bärbel's words pulled Felix from his thoughts, and he returned his attention to the conversation.

Guido cut himself a thick slice off the wheel of cheese. "The Nazis are bad people. They don't care about anything or anyone. You can't imagine how many of my sheep they've stolen and roasted this summer."

"I'm sorry about that." Astrid looked as if she might start crying any moment, confirming Felix's assessment that Bruno's death had deeply shaken her.

"Those fancy fellows in their uniforms think they're above the law." He winked at Felix. "But nobody treats old Guido that way."

After they had told the shepherd about their adventurous experiences, he nodded. "The weather in the mountains can be deceptive. My bones tell me a new cold front is approaching, bringing plenty of snow."

"We were planning to leave early in the morning anyway." Felix drank the hot coffee and grabbed another slice of bread, which he spread thick with lard. Wistfully he thought of Valentina, whose pork lard was legendary—and who must be beside herself with worry. By now, news of Bruno's death had certainly reached the Wallner farm.

"Probably for the best," said Guido, chewing. "Take heart,

the war can't last much longer. Someday humanity will rule in this country again."

With a nod toward Astrid, who had dozed off in her chair in the cozy warmth a while ago, Felix put his knife aside. "What do you think? Should we sleep in the hiding place?"

"Not necessary. No one dares to come up here in the darkness, especially not the border guards who don't know the region well."

"And if they do?"

"Then Balto will warn us."

"Is he up here with you?" Felix hadn't seen the old sheepdog yet and had assumed he was down in the valley with the flock.

"Just like me, he's grown too old for herding sheep." Guido smiled. "Which doesn't stop him from roaming for hours looking for lost lambs. He comes back punctually at nightfall."

As if to confirm his master's words, a short bark sounded outside.

"There he is. I'll let him in." Shortly after, a huge black and brown Bouvier with shaggy winter fur trotted into the cabin, sniffed the guests, and settled under the table.

After dinner, they laid down to sleep on a blanket in front of the stove, while Guido retreated to his bed behind the folding screen, after instructing Balto to keep watch.

The experienced sheepdog lay down in front of the cabin door, his large head on his paws. He seemed to doze off immediately, though one ear remained pricked up.

Reassured, Felix closed his eyes; under Balto's protection, no one would surprise them. He, on the other hand, desperately needed sleep after the ordeals of the last few days. They had another strenuous leg of the journey ahead of them in the morning.

CHAPTER 21

Loud barking tore Bärbel from her sleep. The pale light of dawn filtered through the windows. Beside her, Astrid and Felix bolted upright. Instantly wide awake, they grabbed their now-dried shoes and socks. Everything else had already been stashed in the hiding place the evening before.

Balto stood at the door, emitting a deep, warning growl that made Bärbel's blood freeze in her veins. Thankfully, the massive Bouvier didn't see her as the enemy, instead barking at the people who must be outside.

Guido had gotten up too. After a glance out the window, he stated, "There are three of them. They'll be here in four or five minutes. Get quickly into the hiding place."

Since they had left the trapdoor open, they just needed to slip into the hollow space beneath the floor. Felix jumped in first, then Astrid, and at last Bärbel. Her heart hammered against her ribs as she climbed into the yawning darkness. The musty smell of damp earth and old wood filled her nostrils, mixing with the acrid odor of her fear-induced sweat.

As soon as she crouched into the hip-high space, the old shepherd closed the trapdoor above them. The scraping of the heavy chest he pushed over it made her shudder. For better or worse, they were trapped in absolute darkness, so dense and black Bärbel couldn't see her own hand in front of her face.

Beside her, she heard the shallow breathing of her companions. She had just started fumbling for the bench when a loud knock startled her, answered by Balto's excited barking.

It wasn't long before footsteps crossed the room—presumably Guido on his way to open the door for the border guards. An exchange of words she couldn't understand came next, then heavy boots clomped across the cabin's wooden floor. Bärbel pressed herself into the farthest corner of the tight space, felt the bench against the backs of her knees, and sat down on it, grateful she no longer had to remain in a stooped position.

A wave of air wafted over her cheek from somewhere. She inhaled deeply, greedily. At least she didn't have to fear suffocation.

"Where have you hidden them?"

"What are you looking for?" Guido's voice sounded fearless.

"You know exactly whom we are looking for!" A harsh voice cut through the air. "We know about the two Jews on the run. The man is dead, his companion escaped us. Where is she?"

Bärbel shivered. How did the police know about Astrid? In the next second, she relaxed just a bit. At least they were looking for one woman, not two.

"No woman has been here," Guido replied.

"Oh, really? So why do footprints lead to your cabin?" The mocking voice carried a threatening undertone. Bärbel was tempted to cover her ears, yet her curiosity was stronger.

"They belong to someone from the valley who brought me food. I can show it to you."

"Who was it?"

"Felix Wallner. He promised my son-in-law he'd check on me."

Bärbel clapped her hand over her mouth in horror. Instants later she realized the police must already have determined that Felix was out on a tour.

"Where is he now?"

"Gone. He came by yesterday afternoon, didn't even stay for coffee because he wanted to be back in the village before dark." Guido was as cunning as a fox; he even provided Felix with an alibi for the time of Bruno's death.

"Felix wasn't at his farm or in the village last night."

"You expect me to double-check what he tells me? He's a grown man. Probably has a sweetheart somewhere."

"Don't take me for a fool!" A dull thud echoed through the room, followed by a suppressed groan. Balto barked furiously. A wild scuffle followed, furniture was overturned, glass shattered. To keep from screaming, Bärbel bit down hard on her knuckles, until she tasted blood.

The dog yelped in pain, before silence fell. Just her own heart pounded against her ribs. In the darkness, she fumbled for Astrid's hand, who at some point had settled on the bench next to her. Her fingers were ice-cold and trembling like aspen leaves.

On Bärbel's other side, a warm breath brushed her cheek. Felix pressed his mouth to her ear and whispered, "Don't make a sound, or we're all dead."

As a signal that she had understood, she raised and lowered her head. He seemed to understand because he briefly squeezed her upper arm before moving away. Bärbel passed the instruction on to Astrid in the same way. Above them, dull blows sounded, followed by kicks. Swallowing hard, Bärbel pressed herself against the cool wall, while Astrid nearly crushed her fingers.

"Where is the woman!" a man yelled.

"I know nothing about a woman," Guido responded.

"Liar! Either you tell me what I want to hear, or..." Something crashed with a loud bang.

Bärbel prayed it was merely a piece of wood, but the blood-curdling scream told her otherwise. The border guard had broken one of Guido's bones.

"Ready to tell the truth now, you old fool?" came the mocking challenge, followed by a slap.

"I... know... nothing..." gasped the old shepherd.

Silence descended over the cabin. Just as Bärbel was about to breathe a sigh of relief, two brutal cracks tore through the air. They were followed by a penetrating thud, as if something—no, someone—had fallen to the floor. Once more, she buried her teeth deep into her knuckles to keep from screaming out the violent wave of grief and rage.

She had only known the shepherd for a few hours, yet the thought he might be dead affected her deeply. He didn't deserve to die this way. With all her might, she fought against the overwhelming urge to jump up and hold the perpetrators accountable.

Footsteps clomped above their heads. Undoubtedly, the border police were searching the cabin.

"Hey, boss, we've found a trapdoor!"

Instantly, the blood froze in Bärbel's veins. She sat paralyzed, dreading the moment when their hiding place would be discovered and she would have to look into the faces of Hitler's henchmen. But nothing happened. Felix reached for her free hand and squeezed it reassuringly.

"Is anyone inside?"

"No, just supplies, exactly as the old man claimed."

"Maybe he was telling the truth after all." A brief pause during which the man presumably looked around. "We're leaving. The Jewish fugitive can't have gotten far."

A sob worked its way up Bärbel's throat; she fought hard to swallow it down. Rigid as a stick, she sat in her place, hardly daring to breathe until finally the door slammed shut. Desperate Bärbel whispered: "We need to help Guido."

"We wait," Felix hissed. "First we need to be sure they're gone for good."

"What if he's been shot? We must try to save him!" The thought that Guido might be bleeding out a few meters away while they sat idly in their hiding place was unbearable. She hadn't studied medicine to watch people die virtually before her eyes while she was concerned with her own safety.

After endless minutes of silence, Felix seemed to believe the patrol was far enough away. "Now we can try to get out."

In the absolute darkness, they dared to move to the middle of the space. Tracing the outline of the trapdoor with their fingers, they pushed against it at Felix's command. The heavy chest resting on the trapdoor didn't budge. Gasping, Bärbel pushed and pressed together with the others until her arms trembled. Despite all their effort, the opening became just big enough to push a finger through, nothing more.

Quick-wittedly, Bärbel stuck a pencil she fished from her jacket pocket between the gap before the trapdoor closed again. A beam of light fell into the dungeon, filling it with a tiny hint of dawn.

Bärbel felt an icy hand tightening around her throat. They were trapped in this dark hole, and the only person who knew of their existence was dying—or already dead.

She pictured herself as a withered corpse that would be found years or decades ahead. Her eyes filled with tears, since this definitely wasn't how she wanted to die. Buried alive, miserable, starved to death. Revulsion shook her upper body.

"There's another way out," Felix said into the heavy silence. Bärbel could have thrown her arms around his neck. "A secret tunnel, which leads us back to the surface. The entrance is behind the bench."

All three of them bent down at the same time. Bärbel painfully bumped into someone else's head. Half-dazed, she rubbed her forehead. "Ouch."

"We need light." One didn't need to see Astrid's face to feel her desperation.

"There's a flashlight in my backpack," Felix replied, followed by a groan. "Which is lying somewhere on the mountain."

"What's on the mountain?" Due to the throbbing pain in her temple, Bärbel hadn't caught more than fragments of the conversation between the two.

"My backpack. A candle would help us too."

Bärbel closed her eyes to concentrate better as she pondered why Felix wanted a candle. Then she shrugged; it didn't matter. "I have a flashlight, if that helps."

"Sure, hand it over."

"It's in my backpack. I just need to find it."

"I think it's under the bench," Astrid recalled.

Mindful of the painful collision minutes earlier, Bärbel remained crouched. A shadowy outline moved in front of her. Shortly after, Felix held the backpack in front of her stomach. "Here you go."

It took a while before she managed to open the backpack and rummaged for the flashlight inside. Sweat ran down her back as she handed the flashlight to Felix with trembling hands. Just at that moment, she was seized by a violent cough and dropped the light. It went out a few seconds later.

"Damn it," she cursed.

Felix bent down, pushing her with his backside in the process. Bärbel crouched down and squeezed herself against the shelf, the rough boards digging into her back. In this uncomfortable position, she remained motionless and listened to the rustling and scratching. A gentle click, then the beam of light blinded her as it shone directly into her eyes.

"You found it," she commented unnecessarily.

"Thankfully, it's undamaged." The relief was audible in Felix's voice. He handed Astrid the bedding. "Stash this in some corner so it's not in our way."

Astrid did as she was told, which wasn't an easy feat in the crowded space. As she turned back to Felix with empty hands, he said: "Good. Next, we need to push the bench away from the wall."

It took some contortions before they managed to push the bench to the other side of the hiding place.

Bärbel blew a strand of hair from her face that had come loose from her bun as she rubbed her aching back with both hands.

"Well done," Felix praised. "Guido didn't know if the tunnel was still intact. It hasn't been used in years."

Again, Bärbel felt as if death's bony hand was squeezing her throat. Gasping for air, she bent forward.

"Are you all right?" Audible concern rang in Felix's voice.

"I'm fine." She certainly didn't want to admit that she was terribly afraid of crawling through a pitch-dark, half-collapsed tunnel.

"I'll explore the situation first. You both wait here for me."

"You're going to leave us here?" Despite her panic-inducing fear of the tunnel, she was even more afraid of being left behind without the guide.

"Of course not. But first, I need to find out if the tunnel is still intact. The three of us would just get in each other's way."

"What are we supposed to do in the meantime?" Astrid asked.

"Nothing. Sit on the bench and wait. Once I reach the exit, I'll return to the cabin, push aside the chest and open the trapdoor for you."

Bärbel exhaled slowly. She could wait here, as long as she didn't have to crawl through the dark tunnel.

CHAPTER 22

Felix sent a quick prayer to heaven before taking the flashlight in his mouth. With a hammering heart, he crawled on all fours into the low tunnel. A damp, musty smell filled his nose.

The weak beam of the flashlight cast ghostly shadows on the narrow tunnel walls. He ignored them and concentrated on the path ahead. The light flickered again and again, threatening to go out. The fall had probably caused a loose connection, but he had neither the time nor the light to fix it. So he hoped that both the connection and the batteries would last until they had escaped their underground prison.

Briefly his thoughts drifted to Guido and Balto. He hadn't heard a sound from them since the shots. The hair on the back of his neck stood on end. Guido must have been seriously injured, otherwise he would have freed them from the hiding place. The longer they remained down here, the slimmer the old man's chances of survival became—if he was still alive.

Laboriously, Felix crawled forward. In places the passage was so narrow his shoulders bumped against the walls. A bigger man would have faced serious problems. Swallowing down his fear, he pushed himself forward until he came to a spot with loose soil he needed to remove.

Just where should he put it? He didn't want to push it forward, nor backward in case he needed to crawl back for some reason. Therefore he had no choice but to press the earth firmly into the lower corners of the passageway. Fortunately it hadn't been cold for long, and the earth had not yet frozen deeper than the surface. Nonetheless, his battered fingers itched with cold after just a few minutes of digging.

Once again, he mourned the loss of his backpack, which contained, among various other useful items, a folding shovel for occasions like this when he needed to dig something.

As he worked his way forward slow and steady, his thoughts drifted to his father, who had fled through this tunnel some thirty years earlier, when a gang of robbers had been after him—bandits who had threatened the lives of the hardworking smugglers in the past.

His thoughts promptly wandered to Valentina, imagining how she'd scold him with a disapproving expression: "See what you got yourself into. I told you these Jewish tours are too dangerous. Cobbler, stick to your trade. Move scarce goods across the border; Fritz won't hang you for that."

Of course his sister had been right—she always was—but he still wouldn't listen to her. If he got out of this mess in one piece, he would soon make another Jewish tour. He simply couldn't stop. After all, someone had to help these people. In his mind, he shrugged. If that someone happened to be Felix Wallner, then so be it.

According to his calculations, he had covered about a quarter of the way when he encountered an obstacle. His hands dug deep into the cold, sticky earth. The tunnel had partially collapsed, and the pile of dirt reached almost halfway up its height. Guido hadn't lied when he'd said no one had used the escape route in a long time.

He dug like crazy with his bare hands, pushing the heavy, damp mass aside. Sharp pebbles scraped the skin of his fingertips and pierced the skin beneath his nails. He ignored the pain. Every now and then, he paused in his work to wipe the sweat mixed with dirt from his eyes with his sleeve. To save the flashlight's battery, he turned it off, put it in his jacket pocket and continued digging in the impenetrable darkness.

By now he had lost all sense of time. Minutes might have passed or hours. His arms became leaden, his muscles burned from the unaccustomed activity. Worse than the physical exertion was the stifling air in the narrow tunnel. The lack of oxygen made him short of breath and the work became even more challenging.

Using all his might he shook off the rising panic, and took deep and sustained breaths—even though they filled his lungs with stale, used air that couldn't satisfy his muscles' hunger for oxygen. Undeterred he kept digging, since the responsibility for the lives of the two women weighed heavily on his shoulders.

He absolutely didn't want to die down here like a rat in a trap. Before he could imagine his demise too vividly, he forced himself to focus on the essentials: he had to keep digging, one inch at a time. A minute later his fingers scratched over a sharp stone. As a result, his thumbnail tore deep into the flesh.

Felix clenched his jaw until the wave of pain swept over him, and continued his work. It was almost a blessing that his hands gradually became numb with cold. Stiff and clumsy, he kept digging while simultaneously racking his brain about whether there might be a tool in the hiding place that could be of use. A stabbing cramp shot through his left forearm.

He would never make it with just his bare hands.

Cursing, he crawled backwards into the secret room,

where the women anxiously awaited him. The air here was noticeably better. He lifted his face to the narrow slit of the trapdoor and filled his lungs with the cool, fresh air flowing in. At the same time, he gripped his cramping hand with the other one, stretching it to relieve the cramp.

"What happened?" asked Astrid.

Standing hunched over, he fanned himself thoroughly with cool air before sitting down on the bench. "The tunnel has partially collapsed," he reported, still panting, while rubbing his ice-cold, numb hands. "I estimate about ten meters from here."

Bärbel rummaged in her backpack for gloves and held them out to Felix. "Here, take these."

Felix stared longingly at the thick wool, which he could barely make out in the semi-darkness, then at his hands stiff with dirt. "Thanks for the offer, but they'll just get dirty."

"In our situation that's completely irrelevant. Put them on." Bärbel pressed the gloves against his chest. "At least to warm up. Please."

The gloves barely covered his palms, yet the warm, soft wool was a blessing for his battered hands.

"Will you be able to dig your way through the passage?" asked Bärbel, fiddling with something he couldn't see.

He didn't want to discourage the women, but he also didn't want to lie to them. "I can't say yet. I'm almost through the collapsed section. I can't tell what's behind it."

"I'll take over and you have a break," Astrid offered.

Felix shook his head. "No, I'll do it. Digging in that narrow tunnel is arduous and requires a lot of strength."

"Here, recover your energy first." Bärbel held out a slice of bread and poured water from a bottle into a cup.

He took a greedy gulp to rinse the earthy taste from his mouth, while he mourned for his folding shovel. With that tool, he would manage to move the collapsed earth in no time. "If I had a tool for digging, it would go a lot faster."

"If you give me the flashlight, I'll see if I can find something useful." Astrid stretched out her hand and he placed the light in it, whereupon she searched the room.

"Use it sparingly; I fear the battery won't last much longer."

"Would you like another glass of water?" asked Bärbel.

"Better not. We should be economical with the water. Who knows how long we'll be trapped down here."

"I found something!" cried Astrid, beaming as she swung a metal spoon.

"A spoon?" Bärbel sounded disappointed.

"Better than nothing," grumbled Felix and took the tool, hoping there weren't more collapsed sections in the tunnel. After he had eaten the bread, he returned the gloves and squeezed back into the passage, the spoon between his teeth, the flashlight in his hand.

In the beam, he saw that he had almost completely removed the heap of earth. His heart leaped with joy because he could not see any further obstacles behind it. At least the next ten meters or so, which were illuminated by the flashlight, seemed intact.

The spoon was definitely not ideal for digging, but at least more effective than working with bare hands. Systematically, he cleared away the pile, pressing the crumbs of earth firmly into the corners to avoid clogging the tunnel even more. With each spoonful of earth he pushed aside, his hope grew that he might succeed in reaching the exit. Every few minutes he had to pause, shake his hand, and gasp for air—no matter how stale and used up it was. He didn't want to be forced to crawl back into the hiding place a second time.

His arms and shoulders became numb, his knees ached from the uneven ground, but he forced himself to continue.

Further and further. Spoonful by spoonful, he made his way until he had cleared the buried section.

"Finally," he muttered and crawled on. For now, he and the two women were safe: the border guards had withdrawn after discovering the secret storage room under the table. But they might return and search the cabin thoroughly again or even set the wooden structure on fire.

An icy shiver raced down his back. Although the earth didn't burn, he dared not imagine whether and how far the flames would reach into the tunnel if the fire greedily consumed the wooden cabin. If they didn't die in the heat, they would suffocate miserably because the flames would suck all the oxygen from the air.

Haste was in order. So he crawled, shoveled and pressed on, driven by the desperate desire to see daylight on the other side of the tunnel, about thirty meters away.

To save the battery, he kept turning the flashlight off and moving forward in absolute darkness. Eventually, his hands struck something hard.

His heart skipped a beat. A boulder would mean the end of their escape—and probably their lives. Cautiously, he felt his way forward. Relief flooded through him as he sensed a smooth wooden surface. This had to be the exit. "I made it through!"

He illuminated the wooden door with the flashlight. His euphoria vanished.

"Damn it..."

A massive padlock adorned the bolt. The disappointment hit him like a punch to the gut. He wanted nothing more than to curl up into a sobbing ball, never to get up again. So close to the goal and now this!

He pulled and tugged, struck it several times with the spoon, but the accursed lock didn't budge. Rusted on the outside, the locking mechanism seemed to have defied the humidity. Damp earth trickled down his neck, underscoring the desperation of his situation. The flashlight flickered threatening to go out, so he switched it off again. He had no choice but to crawl all the way back and bring the women the bad news.

Their escape was over.

If the border patrol didn't find them, the Grim Reaper would.

CHAPTER 23

"Do you think he made it?" Astrid asked. Usually she wasn't afraid of enclosed spaces, but the long wait in the dark dungeon was getting to her.

"Definitely. Otherwise he would have been back by now."

Astrid desperately wanted to believe Bärbel; the alternative was simply too horrific to even consider. Images of dried-up corpses, excavated decades in the future, appeared in her mind. Nausea worked its way up her throat, and she gagged several times. Under no circumstances could she allow herself to throw up down here.

The next moment, Felix's backside appeared in the tunnel opening. He awkwardly turned around before saying in a sepulchral voice: "There's a padlock at the exit."

"Oh my God, we're doomed." Bärbel's voice broke off. "What should we do?"

Felix remained silent. He, who had always been confident over the past few days, seemed to have no answer to that question.

Astrid pulled herself together. "I could try to open it."

"I already did that. It's locked tight, even though it's badly rusted on the outside." Felix's voice sounded defeated.

"Perhaps I can pick the lock."

"You?" Bärbel's voice was full of surprise.

"Where did you learn that?" Felix asked.

"From my brothers." Astrid felt the need to justify herself. "The life of a Jewish family hasn't been easy in recent years. You end up doing things you wouldn't do under normal circumstances."

Bärbel's jaw dropped. Felix, on the other hand, kept his composure. "Still waters run deep. It's definitely worth a try."

"I'll need a hairpin." Astrid turned to Bärbel and pointed at her bun. However, the woman didn't seem to be listening. "Bärbel?"

Bärbel flinched. "Yes, what is it?"

"I asked if I could have a hairpin."

"A..." Bärbel looked at her in confusion, even as her hand felt for her bun, from which several strands of hair had come loose. She pulled out a hairpin and handed it to Astrid.

As Astrid felt the hard metal between her fingers, she became fully aware of the responsibility resting on her shoulders. If she didn't manage to pick the lock... She shuddered, closed her eyes, and concentrated on her breathing.

After a while, Felix asked: "Are you ready?"

No! "Yes."

He orchestrated the position change in the cramped hideout until Astrid was kneeling in front of the tunnel entrance with sweaty hands. Felix pressed the flashlight into her hand. "You'll need this. Good luck!"

Astrid swallowed the lump in her throat. The thought of crawling through the narrow tunnel was bad enough, let alone doing it alone with the responsibility of picking the lock so they wouldn't die down here. Panic paralyzed her. She didn't want to be alone at any cost. "A-a-aren't you coming with me?"

"It's too narrow for two. I couldn't help you anyway."

"Please." She turned to face him. "I'm afraid to be alone in the tunnel and when I'm afraid, my hands shake. Which means, I won't be able to pick the lock."

"If it makes you feel better, I'll come with you."

"Thank you."

"I don't want to stay behind on my own," Bärbel squeaked.

"Fine," Felix grumbled. "One person more or less doesn't make a difference. Bärbel brings up the rear."

"What about our backpacks?" asked Bärbel.

Felix scratched his head, causing dust and dirt to trickle onto his shoulders. "They'll only get in our way in the narrow tunnel. We'll leave them here and return for them later."

"We need to go back to the cabin anyway to check on Guido." Bärbel seemed to have regained her composure.

Shaken, Astrid bit her lip. Wallowing in her own misery, she had completely forgotten about the old shepherd.

"Let's get going." Felix gently pushed her into the tunnel.

The pitch-black opening seemed like a dragon's maw, waiting to devour her whole. "Dragons aren't real," she murmured to encourage herself. "Monsters, ghosts, none of them exist. Only the Nazis—they're the ones to fear."

Laboriously, she crawled forward on all threes, clutching the flashlight tightly with her free hand. She constantly fought against the impulse to stop. She couldn't go back anyway because Felix was right behind her. Lying in the passage like a toddler throwing a tantrum wasn't an option either, so the only way was forward. With each yard, the air became stuffier. The musty stench made her gag. Every breath was a struggle.

She thought of her brothers. If they were here with her,

she'd be just as afraid, but she'd rather bite off her tongue than show weakness by giving up. Just as she had regained some semblance of control, something soft and sticky brushed her cheek.

A stifled scream escaped her, her hand jerked up and the flashlight slipped from her trembling fingers. The light flickered before it went out. Absolute darkness surrounded her. She could almost grasp the darkness settling heavily on her chest, squeezing the air from her lungs. Tears burned in her eyes, flowing freely down her cheeks. She was trapped inside this black hell.

"Astrid?" Felix's muffled voice reached her. "Everything will be fine. You can do this. The exit can't be much farther."

She pulled herself up on his words as if they were a hanging ladder and wiped the tears from her face. She could do this. Blind in the dark she crawled forward until her head hit a hard surface.

"I think I'm knocked against the door," she said and fumbled for the padlock with sweaty, clammy hands. It didn't take long until her fingers sensed rusty metal.

A spark of hope warmed her from within. Tiny rays of light seeped through hair-thin cracks in the old wood, just enough to make the outline of the lock visible. Her teeth clenched tight, she took the lock into her hand, turning it this way and that until she could guess the locking mechanism.

In principle, it's no different in the dark than in the light, once you've found the entrance, she encouraged herself. Her right hand grabbed the hairpin, secured on her head. Her breath came in bursts. Four times she tried to insert the pin into the lock, four times she failed—not because of poor visibility, but because her hands were shaking so badly.

On the verge of tears, she leaned against the wall. "I can't do it."

"Yes, you can," Felix's calm voice said. "Close your eyes and take a deep breath."

She followed his instructions.

"Now, imagine the lock. Go through each movement you need to make until you've opened it."

Astrid didn't know how that would help, but since she had no better ideas, she did as she was told. Twice she went through the complete process in her mind. When she opened her eyes again, the tiny rays of light seemed brighter than before. With renewed confidence, she took the padlock in her hand a second time and positioned the hairpin. As if by magic, the tip slid into the mechanism—just as she had practiced hundreds of times under the critical eyes of her brothers.

Hope flooded her body. Carefully, she felt her way forward, sensing every little resistance, every click of the springs. Endless seconds—or minutes—passed, during which only the scratching of metal on metal could be heard. Her fingers became completely steady, working automatically, almost without her conscious contribution, as if they had a memory of their own.

Finally she heard a satisfying click. The mechanism gave way, and the shackle of the lock swung open. A feeling of triumph warmed her from head to toe.

"I did it!" she called out.

"Great!" Felix praised. "Can you open the door?"

She pushed, pressed, squeezed, threw herself against it. The door didn't move a millimeter. The joyful excitement within her melted like the meager remains of a snowman in the spring sun.

"It's not moving at all." Her voice resonated with despair. They were so close to freedom, just this door separated them from the surface. If she managed to open it.

"Did you push it?" came Felix's voice from behind.

"Yes." Leading with her shoulder, she threw herself against the door, ignoring the stabbing pain that shot through her body. The wooden planks vibrated under her weight, yet the door didn't move an inch. She could have screamed in frustration.

"Then try pulling."

"Pulling?" The excitement of the last few hours, the darkness and the fear had clouded her mind. Felix's words made no sense. She stared at the door as if it were an unsolvable puzzle.

Patiently, he repeated: "Pull the door toward you."

Realization hit her like lightning. *Of course!* She was on the verge of hysterical laughter. All her strength had been wasted pushing the door in the wrong direction. She felt for the edge, dug her fingertips between wood and earth. With a strong pull, the door swung open, and Astrid tumbled backward against Felix.

"Not so stormy, young lady." The relief was audible in his voice.

After dust, dirt and cobwebs had cleared, fresh air as well as weak daylight penetrated the dark tunnel.

"You need to go first." Felix nudged her, since the tunnel was far too narrow for him to overtake her. When she hesitated, he gently repeated: "Go on ahead now."

Astrid mustered her courage and hoisted herself up into a kind of rock crevice whose boundaries she couldn't see, since it took a while for her eyes to adjust to the brightness. Finally she recognized that the entrance to the tunnel was hidden under a snowdrift.

While Felix and Bärbel were still on their way up, she began to shovel the soft snow aside. Soon enough her fingers went numb from the cold. Yet, she shoveled tirelessly, not noticing how Felix and Bärbel joined her on the right and left.

Suddenly her hand hit emptiness. A hole gaped in the snow wall, and she peered out into the blazing sun.

"We made it," she whispered, overwhelmed by the beautiful sight of the winter landscape. She lifted her face to the brilliant blue sky, filling her lungs with fresh, cold mountain air. A smile on her lips, she savored the sweet taste of freedom.

Then her gaze fell on her companions, whose blissful expressions didn't match their soaked and dirty appearance at all. After a few minutes, during which the sun warmed their stiff limbs and infused them with new vitality, Felix destroyed the happy mood.

"The danger isn't over. We need to erase all traces of our presence at the cabin and tackle the final leg to the border."

"And we need to check on Guido, maybe we'll reach him in time to help," added Bärbel.

CHAPTER 24

Taking a large leap, Bärbel jumped onto a stone by the outhouse standing directly next to the exit, while Felix closed the wooden door to the secret passage. From there, she followed the existing footprints to the cabin, making sure not to leave new tracks in the snow.

The cabin door swung in the wind—the pursuers hadn't bothered to close it when they'd rushed away. Anxiety bearing down on her, she followed Felix inside. The table had been pushed aside, revealing an open trapdoor.

"There's blood," Astrid croaked and walked around the trapdoor pointing upright into the room. "Oh, how terrible!"

Bärbel barely managed to spring forward in time to catch Astrid, who collapsed in a faint. Gently, she lowered Astrid to the floor and propped her legs up against the table.

A few steps away, Felix was leaning over Guido's lifeless form. Next to him lay his faithful sheepdog Balto, his brown fur stained red. A heart-wrenching whimper reached her ears.

Although Bärbel was accustomed to seeing horrific things due to her internship at the field hospital, she had to swallow several times at the sight of the massacre that had happened here. The old shepherd appeared to have been dead for some time. Nevertheless, she bent down to take his pulse. His neck under her hand felt cold and hard; rigor mortis had set in.

"He's dead," she whispered.

"What should we do with Balto?" Felix seemed as shocked by the sight of the suffering dog as she was.

Bärbel turned toward the injured animal. Although she had no experience with sick animals, she could tell at first glance that Balto was dying. His large, intelligent eyes had turned glassy, and he didn't even move his head when she petted him.

There was nothing she could do for him except comfort him in his final minutes. She squatted next to the large animal in a cross-legged position and carefully placed his head on her lap. Felix looked at her with dread in his eyes. A groan told Bärbel that Astrid must have regained consciousness.

"Could you please look after Astrid?" she asked Felix. "Give her something to drink. She shouldn't get up yet."

Then she returned her attention to Balto, whose brown eyes looked at her with an almost human sadness. His flanks rose and fell in shallow, irregular breaths.

"Good boy," she whispered, as her fingers gently stroked his fur. "Brave dog."

The minutes passed, the whimpering grew quieter, his breathing became shallower. A final, deep sigh moved his body before he went limp in her arms. The faithful brown eyes stared lifelessly at his dead master. Tears ran down Bärbel's cheeks, dripping onto his blood-encrusted fur. Eventually, she pulled herself together and laid his head next to that of the old shepherd.

"Now you're together again." Barely holding herself together, she stood up and looked around for Astrid, who was no longer lying on the floor. There was no trace of her or

Felix. For a terrifying second, she feared the two had left without her.

Giving a deep sigh, she scolded herself for the absurd idea and walked across the room. Next to the trapdoor behind the folding screen stood the two backpacks neatly arranged, but still no sign of the pair.

Seconds later the door creaked. Startled, Bärbel was about to crawl under the bed when she saw Felix enter the room.

"How is Balto?" asked Astrid.

"He died." Once more Bärbel's eyes filled with tears.

"It's already past noon, it might be better to wait until tomorrow morning," Felix suggested.

"I won't stay here a single minute longer. Not with..." Astrid cast a disturbed glance at the pool of blood next to Guido's body.

Bärbel didn't like the idea of spending another night in the cabin either, but it had nothing to do with the dead, rather with the living. "Staying here is far too risky. The border guards probably won't return today, but definitely tomorrow. You know the Nazis, once they've tasted blood, they don't give up. They'll systematically comb through the entire region to find the Jewish refugee."

Felix rubbed his unshaven face, looking old and tired. "It's a four-hour march to St. Antönierjoch, more if it has snowed along the way."

"I don't care how long it takes. I'm not staying here," Astrid was quick to assure him.

Felix leaned against the table, his face turned away from the dead shepherd. "The issue is we need to be up there before the guards change at six in the evening, otherwise we'll miss the bribed border guards and have to spend the night outdoors."

"That's still five and a half hours from now. We'll definitely make it." Bärbel was confident she had enough reserves for the distance, though Astrid's condition worried he, since she had just fainted and had limped on the short way from the cabin door to the chair. "Are you sure you can make it?"

"One hundred percent. I've endured so much already, I'll manage the rest too." Astrid brushed a strand of hair from her forehead.

"What do you think, Felix? Should we risk it?" Bärbel wanted to leave the decision to him; after all, he was the mountain guide who knew the area like the back of his hand.

He moved his head back and forth. "Under normal circumstances, I'd wait until tomorrow. But there's nothing normal about this tour. Bärbel is right. The danger that a patrol will return and turn over every stone looking for us is too great. By then, you must be in Switzerland, otherwise God help us all."

"It's decided, then." Bärbel looked Felix directly in the eyes. "I'll dress Astrid's knee before we set off."

"And I'll see if I can find anything useful. Guido certainly wouldn't mind." Felix retrieved a rough cloth backpack from the coat rack and began his search.

"Do you happen to have a miracle cure for blisters, too?" asked Astrid.

"Let me see." When Astrid took off her socks, Bärbel let out a gasp. "Good heavens, that looks awful! Why didn't you say something sooner?"

"I didn't want to complain."

"You really should have told me, I can see your raw flesh. Let those wounds air out while I look for bandages." It didn't take long before she found Guido's first aid kit. As she bandaged Astrid's knee and sore feet, she observed from the corner of her eye how Felix refilled the water bottles, packed crampons and a folding shovel, and replaced the flashlight batteries with new ones. Just before he tied up the backpack, he put in a small hand mirror.

That seemed rather vain to her, so she asked, "What do you need a mirror for?"

"Old smuggler's trick," explained Felix. "You can use it to make signals by catching the sun, much better than even a flashlight."

"Oh." She gaped in amazement. This man was cunning as a fox. "I'd like to bury Guido and his dog."

"We mustn't." He shook his head. "If the border police return, nothing should indicate that we've been here."

Bärbel swallowed the lump in her throat. "I hadn't thought of that."

A few minutes later Bärbel cast a final glance at the dead, the three shouldered their backpacks and set off.

They had been walking for about half an hour when an explosion shattered the silence. Bärbel stopped mid-step, anxiously peering in all directions. "Someone shot at us!"

"That wasn't a shot, it was an explosion. Probably the patrol blowing up a cave or a rock to smoke us out." Felix pursed his lips. "In this weather, that's pure madness."

"Why?" asked Astrid.

"Because of the fresh snow, there's always the danger of an avalanche."

Astrid visibly relaxed. "I see. Fortunately, avalanches are very rare."

Felix opened his mouth as if to contradict her, but closed it again. Bärbel watched as he examined the surrounding slopes with narrowed eyes. His nervous tension transferred to Bärbel, and she chewed on her lower lip. When nothing happened, he gave the signal to move on. "We need to hurry to reach the pass on time."

About ten minutes later, a second explosion tore through the silence. Again they stopped. Bärbel looked at the opposite slope. The snow covered the mountain like a sparkling white blanket. The echo of the explosion faded away until total silence descended over the landscape once more.

Just as she turned toward Felix, she heard a distant rumble. It was so faint she thought it might just be the after effect in her ears. Within seconds though, the rumble swelled like thunder in the distance, deep and booming. Unlike thunder, however, it did not fade, but grew louder and louder. In a many-voiced echo, it reverberated off the rock faces.

"Holy Mary, Mother of God!" Felix's face had turned ashen. Above the noise, he barked, "Avalanche! We need to run!"

Bärbel still couldn't see anything, though she stared spellbound at the undisturbed blanket of snow on the opposite slope. A second later something broke loose. A small crack appeared in the snow, gradually growing larger.

Felix grabbed her arm and urged her on. "We need to get higher. It's not safe here." He had barely finished speaking when the white mass broke loose. There was no stopping it now.

Bärbel couldn't comprehend what was happening around her. Thanks to Felix's unforgiving grip, she stumbled up the path.

"Faster!" Felix drove her on mercilessly as she fell, picked herself up again, and stumbled on.

Using hands and feet, she climbed up the slope, painfully scraping her shin against a sharp edge. In her haste to move forward, her jacket caught on something, tearing a hole into the fabric.

Gradually, the fog in Bärbel's brain cleared. With sharpened senses, she perceived her surroundings. Astrid was marching a few steps ahead of her in the same frantic hurry, while Felix brought up the rear of their small caravan.

From the corner of her eye, she watched as the slow descent of the avalanche became faster, bigger, more dangerous with each second.

Gasping, she hastened upward, as the avalanche thundered down the slope on the other side of the valley, carrying away everything in its path: trees, rocks, nothing escaped its crushing force.

"It should be safe up here," Felix finally determined as they reached a plateau.

By now, the noise was deafening. Bärbel covered her ears because she felt like her head might explode. From their vantage point, she watched, captivated, the spectacle of this enormous natural disaster, which was beautiful in its eerie way.

"Are you sure nothing can happen to us here?" Astrid squeaked next to her.

"Pretty sure." Felix didn't seem overly concerned, so Bärbel relaxed. In his presence, she felt safe. The mountain-experienced man surely wasn't witnessing an avalanche for the first time in his life.

A thunderous roar, accompanied by sharp cracking and bursting, drowned out every other sound. Even on the distant plateau where they stood, the ground vibrated with such intensity Bärbel thought she was standing next to one of those vibrating machines used to level road surfaces.

The entire mountain, as well as the surrounding mountains, seemed to tremble under the primal force. Her hands shook in the same rhythm, her gaze magnetically drawn toward the masses of snow. They seemed to have risen into a living being: a merciless dervish shooting into the valley and destroying everything that stood in its way. She didn't want to imagine what would happen if the swirling snow masses were pushed up the slope where she was standing.

The cold wind ahead of the avalanche hit her face and constricted her throat. With it came a sharp, biting smell—a mixture of fresh snow, ground ice and the dust of broken stones. A metallic taste reminiscent of blood settled on her tongue.

Without wanting to, Bärbel began to scream. In panic, she was about to run for her very life, until a heavy hand rested on her shoulder. Felix shouted in her ear: "This is the safest place for us."

How she wanted to believe him! Witnessing the natural disaster made her realize how small and insignificant she was. Even the united mankind of the world would be powerless to stop this avalanche. Once more, the slope trembled beneath her feet. The dull vibration reverberated through her marrow and bone.

Undeterred by its observers, the avalanche continued to rage, leaving behind a swath of destruction. Finally, the snow masses plunged over one last ledge before rolling with brute force into the valley floor. Bärbel felt the impact deep in her bones. After that, time seemed to stand still. The rapid snow masses lost their momentum, slowly eating their way through the valley.

A huge cloud of snow, dust and ice rose into the air, veiling the sky and bathing the sun in a pale light gray. From the previously cloudless sky, snow crystals trickled down onto Bärbel, until a thick white layer covered her face, clothes and hands.

She wiped the flakes from her eyes without taking her gaze off the avalanche that continued to fill the valley. Slowly it rumbled toward the shepherd's cabin, whose dark wooden walls gave a stark contrast against the whiteness of its surroundings.

Bärbel's breath caught at the notion that they had been there less than an hour ago. Anxiously chewing on her lower lip, her eyes followed the deadly mass of snow, ice, and debris. Down there lay Guido and his faithful companion Balto, united in death. But the avalanche knew no mercy—or did it intend to give the dead a dignified grave after all?

Infinitely slow, the roof burst under the pressure of the first wave of snow. Within a short time, the cabin's shattered remains disappeared beneath the approaching monster. Only the chimney stuck out of the snow, like a building block left there by a giant at play.

It seemed as if the cabin's destruction had robbed the avalanche of its strength. It pushed the wooden remains a little further along before finally coming to a halt just inches from the outhouse.

The thundering roar ended abruptly, as if nature had decided to hold its breath. An eerie silence descended over the landscape. Her throat parched, Bärbel gazed at the bizarre snow cover beneath which lay buried the winding path they had walked less than an hour ago. Together with the shepherd's cabin, a rock outcrop behind it had also disappeared, revealing an unexpected view of distant peaks.

Gradually, the swirling snow cloud settled. Bärbel choked on the metallic-tasting air as she brushed the dust from her clothing.

"We need to move," Felix urged.

"What about Guido?" Horror was written all over Astrid's face.

"He got his burial after all." Bärbel was surprised at her own cold-hearted remark. It was as if the avalanche had buried her emotions, leaving behind nothing but a numb shell.

"At least the border guards can't follow our tracks anymore." Felix seemed to be suffering from the same emotional shock as Bärbel.

CHAPTER 25

Felix wiped the dust from his face with his sleeve. The avalanche had affected him more than he wanted to admit. He tried not to show it in front of the women, though his heart was still racing. They had been incredibly lucky, having left behind both Guido's cabin and the valley when the catastrophe started.

From Guido's cabin, the border crossing at Gafierjoch was closer than the one at St. Antönierjoch, which was the reason why the Nazi bastards had detonated the slope on the other side. Felix shuddered. Several times he had considered changing the route, just the uncertainty had stopped him.

The border guards at St. Antönierjoch were expecting two refugees; they had already received a down payment. Nothing should go wrong there. Felix had no idea who was currently on duty at Gafierjoch or whether that person could be bribed to look the other way when the two women crossed the border illegally, leaving the German Reich.

He had chosen the longer but safer path. In hindsight, it had been the perfect decision. Still, chills raced down his spine as he realized that this—rather insignificant—decision had saved their lives. If they had been on their way to Gafierjoch, the avalanche would have caught them in the middle of the slope, and they wouldn't have had a prayer of escaping.

No one survived a monster avalanche like the one they'd just experienced. Even if by some lucky coincidence they weren't crushed they would suffocate miserably under meters of snow if they weren't found quickly enough. And no one would have searched for them. He shuddered again, before he forced the doubts aside.

The avalanche had cost them a lot of time. Valuable minutes, which they needed to reach the border before the changing of the guards. He didn't want to spend the night in the open under any circumstances—in constant danger of being caught, literally on the final stretch. A horrific notion occurred to him with sudden urgency.

"What day is today?" he asked.

"I think Thursday," Astrid answered.

"No, it's Friday." Bärbel counted on her fingers, "I set off for the cave on Tuesday, you arrived there on Wednesday, when that terrible storm was raging."

Felix flinched. It had been less than two days since Bruno had walked among them.

"That's right," Astrid chimed in. "We continued to Guido's cabin on Thursday, which means today must be Friday."

"Damn it all to hell!" Felix blurted out.

"Another problem?" Astrid's nose tip stood out pale against her face, which was reddened from exertion and sunshine.

"We need to hurry." He wanted to spare them the bitter truth. But after a look at their exhausted expressions, he changed his mind. Perhaps the bad news would help them mobilize their energy reserves. "The two bribed border guards are on duty until tonight, then they're returning to the valley for two weeks."

"Which means today is our last chance to escape." Bärbel pressed her lips into a thin line.

"If we don't pick up the pace, our chances to be there on time are slim," he urged the visibly tired women. Even for him, the speed was challenging.

If they didn't make it in time, he didn't know what to do with the two of them. They couldn't go back to the village. Guido's cabin was destroyed, the cave near Gargellen likely discovered and spending the night in the open was far too dangerous. As a last resort, he considered taking them home with him and hiding them there. He groaned. Valentina would make his life hell for endangering the entire family.

After about half an hour, Astrid stumbled and fell flat on her face. Felix immediately rushed to her side to help her up. The deep despair in her eyes stabbed at his heart, so he lied, "It's not much farther."

"Really?" A spark of hope lit up her face.

"We've made good time, so we can allow ourselves a five-minute break." He took off his backpack and rummaged for the bread and cheese he had packed at Guido's. Suddenly he saw the face of the dead shepherd hoovering before him. *I didn't want to steal from you, I'll pay it back.* The vision disappeared. Felix scolded himself for being foolish. First, Guido was dead and didn't need food anymore, and second, the cabin with all its belongings had meanwhile been buried under the avalanche. The old shepherd would certainly not mind the living benefiting from his food.

He cut generous slices and handed them to the women. After eating and drinking water from their bottles, Astrid said, even before he had given the signal to depart, "I feel much better already. We can continue."

"It's going to be tough once we have to climb that last

slope over there." Felix pointed to a steep ascent with a hut at the top. Despite squinting his eyes, the distance was too far to distinguish it, yet Felix knew a swastika flag was flying on its roof. "The hut you see up there stands directly at the border."

They continued in single file: Felix in front, setting the pace, Astrid in the middle, and Bärbel taking up the rear. Every few minutes, he checked whether the women managed to keep up with his murderous pace. At each glance back, the total exhaustion was etched deeper into their faces, their steps were heavier, their shoulders more hunched. However they struggled on without complaint—undoubtedly driven by the fear of being arrested. The Gestapo was an excellent motivator.

The final climb up to the pass seemed endless; again and again, the small group paused, gasping for air. Felix had chosen the shortcut over the steep slope—a risky maneuver—because it saved twenty valuable minutes of travel time.

Exactly ten minutes before the changing of the guards, they approached the border station from behind. Felix motioned for Astrid and Bärbel to hide behind a boulder. Full of admiration for their tenacity, he caught his breath for a couple of moments before greeting the guards.

Meinhold and Christoph stood smoking in front of the entrance to their shelter, their rifles shouldered casually. They had probably seen him for a while and gave a brief nod.

"No one here but us," Christoph said without preamble.

"You give us the rest of the money, and the couple can pass without inspection," Meinhold added.

Felix inhaled deeply. "There's been a slight change of plan. There are two women instead of a couple."

Christoph's expression darkened. "That wasn't the agreement."

Felix's mind raced. "It makes no difference to you. I announced two people, you let two people cross."

The two border guards exchanged glances. Meinhold scratched his chin. "This doesn't happen to have anything to do with the Jew who was shot near Gargellen, does it?"

"I don't know anything about that," Felix lied without batting an eyelid. He put his hand in his trouser pocket, showing the agreed upon money. "At the meeting point, there were two women; the man didn't make it out of Vienna."

"And miraculously, a second woman appeared instead?" Christoph was still skeptical, which didn't stop him from grabbing the banknotes, which quickly disappeared in his pocket.

"They met during the train journey. But the details are none of your business. You've got your money." Felix mustered his calm. The guards exchanged glances once more. Felix knew the game; they were trying to squeeze more money out of him.

"The captured Jew has made business more dangerous," Meinhold drawled. "The Gestapo has issued a search warrant for a Jewish woman."

"Which considerably increases the risk." Christoph took a step closer. "For all of us."

"Well, it's a good thing I have two women with me, isn't it?" Felix wanted to keep the additional bribe as small as possible.

Christoph scratched the back of his head. "Still. We'll be in hot water if the Gestapo suspects something."

Meinhold seemed to have had enough of the negotiation. "Do they want to cross into Switzerland or not? Our shift ends in a few minutes."

"How much do you want?" Felix intended to force them to show their cards.

"What do you have to offer?" Meinhold smirked.

"A Swiss pocketknife." Felix pulled his favorite knife from

his jacket. Extra slow, he dangled it in front of Meinhold's nose, knowing the border guard collected knives of all kinds.

A greedy gleam entered Meinhold's eyes. As he stretched out his hand for the knife, Felix moved it out of reach. "You'll get it once the women have crossed the border, not a minute sooner."

"All right. Tell them to hurry."

Felix breathed out in relief. "I'll get them."

CHAPTER 26

Astrid crouched next to Bärbel behind the flat boulder, waiting for Felix's return. She could hardly wait to take the last steps toward freedom. Although the border wasn't marked on the ground, she imagined how she would leap elegantly over an imaginary red line into Switzerland and make faces at the border guards from a safe distance.

Or perhaps she should skip the face-making. The Nazis might be capable of crossing into Swiss territory to haul her back. Her gaze fell on Bärbel, who was staring with a gloomy expression at the steep path they had climbed up.

"What's wrong? Aren't you excited?" she asked.

Bärbel jumped as if she had forgotten Astrid was sitting beside her. "Yes, I am..."

"But?" Astrid couldn't fathom why the other woman seemed less than elated.

"Do you think our escape was worth it?"

"Of course. Sure, it was exhausting and nerve-wracking and terrifying. But all that is behind us, now that we're at the border and will be free in just a few minutes. Even the scratches and bloody blisters on my feet will heal soon. Then nothing will remain to remind us of this ordeal." Astrid had been gritting her teeth with every step during the last hour, as her weeping blisters rubbed against the soaked leather of her worn-out shoes.

"That's not what I mean." Bärbel thoughtfully wrapped a strand of hair around her finger.

"What exactly is bothering you?"

Bärbel looked at her with pain-filled eyes. "The old shepherd and his dog died because of us. If we hadn't sought shelter with them, they would still be alive."

"You mustn't think that way. The Nazis are to blame; they're the ones who killed them." Since Bruno's death, which had deeply shocked her, Astrid had had plenty of time to mull things over. Of course she mourned the friendly old man and his dog, but there was nothing she could do about it. "Guido was aware of how dangerous his actions were. Do you remember he even told us that?"

When Bärbel didn't respond, she continued: "It was his own decision. He didn't have to hide us. He did it because he hated the Nazis and wanted to help. It has worked just fine for many years, however not this time. It wasn't our fault. We didn't do anything wrong."

"If we had covered our tracks better, maybe the patrol wouldn't have searched his cabin and wouldn't have killed him..." Bärbel was shaken by sobs. "... he would still be alive."

"There's no point in worrying about what you could have done differently. We have to live with how things turned out." Astrid placed a hand on Bärbel's shoulder. "Guido's death is not your fault, nor Felix's or mine. Sometimes life is simply unfair and cruel."

"I don't want it to be!" Bärbel snapped like a small child.

"Nobody wants that, but we can't change fate, we can just

try to make the best of it." How often had Astrid been annoyed by these wise words from her mother? However in the last few days she had recognized the truth in them, and was using the same words to comfort Bärbel.

A heart-wrenching moan was the answer.

"You have to look forward, to your new life in Switzerland." Astrid frantically racked her brain how she could help Bärbel overcome her guilt. "Just think how much you can do once you are there. Establishing contact with escape helpers, organizing accommodations, collecting money—I'm sure there are a thousand things you can do."

"Do you really think so?" Bärbel's mouth twitched upward.

"As sure as I'm sitting here."

The next moment, Bärbel's eyebrows contorted into a sullen grimace. "I haven't paid my share of the bribe. With my luck, they won't let me cross anyway."

"You didn't lose the silver necklace, did you?"

Bärbel shook her head. "Felix said it wasn't valuable enough."

Astrid desperately wanted to instill some confidence in her new friend. "My offer still stands. If all else fails, I'll give the border guards my mother's golden wedding ring."

"I can't accept that."

"Of course you can. Once we're in Switzerland, I won't need it anymore. I'll stay with one of my mother's friends." Astrid didn't mention that she still had to find this friend, and it wasn't certain that she would take her in.

It was obvious that Bärbel was struggling with herself. Finally, she nodded: "But I'll pay back every penny the ring is worth."

"That's exactly what we'll do." The main value of the ring wasn't material but sentimental. No one could replace that. Nevertheless, she didn't regret her offer. Mother had sacrificed the ring to buy Astrid's life; she would agree if it was used to save Bärbel's life instead.

Footsteps crunched in the snow and Felix appeared.

"They'll let us through," he said tersely. "We need to hurry; the shift change is about to happen any minute."

Bärbel rose with hesitation. "What price do they want for me?"

Astrid glanced anxiously at Felix; for a terrifying moment she feared the ring wouldn't be enough.

Not a muscle moved in his weather-beaten face. "I've already taken care of the bribe."

"How?" stammered Bärbel.

"I paid for two people. The border guards don't care who those two people are."

Seeing how Bärbel's eyes filled with tears, Astrid fought against the lump in her throat, fondly remembering their benefactor Bruno, who had so generously given her the place of his missing companion, before he had been murdered on the snowy slope.

The realization that Bruno was another dead person who had paved their way to freedom hit her with the force of an uppercut. Her first impulse was to give up crossing the border. It felt as if she was literally stepping over corpses. She couldn't bear that. How could she look in the mirror every day if her new life in freedom was built on the backs of others?

Then she remembered her own words: She couldn't help the dead anymore, couldn't change fate, but she could make the best of it. She pulled herself together and followed Felix to the border post. At the sight of the two uniformed border guards, her knees almost gave out, since she feared something might go wrong at the last second.

But everything went smoothly. The two guards waved them past without even glancing at their papers. Next they raised the barrier. Astrid couldn't resist giving a little hop of joy as she crossed the border.

"What are you doing?" asked Felix, who had observed her.

"I'm celebrating crossing the border."

He laughed good-naturedly. "Right now we're in no-man's-land between the two countries; Switzerland is over there."

Astrid swallowed hard. Hopefully her premature hop hadn't jinxed the situation. It would be a catastrophe if the Swiss border officials didn't let her into the country. She would be trapped in no-man's-land, like a ghost doomed to haunt the site of its earthly suffering for all eternity.

"Can something still go wrong?" she asked in a thin voice.

"Nah," he grinned. "The Swiss aren't half as strict, except with Jews, but since neither you nor Bärbel are Jewish... He made a hand gesture to show how little risk was involved.

"Phew. That's a relief." The next moment she thought of Bruno. "What about Bruno and Martha? You originally wanted to smuggle them across the border, and they're both Jewish." *Were*, she corrected herself mentally. Bruno was no longer among the living. As for the mysterious Martha, it was at least questionable.

"That's true. Anyway the two officials on duty this week are decent men." Felix's assessment would prove to be correct.

Her heart pounding Astrid handed the Swiss official her mother's passport, featuring the forged birth date.

After giving it a superficial glance, he asked: "What is the purpose of your trip to Switzerland?"

She looked at him, bewildered, before answering: "I'm visiting a family friend in Lucerne."

"Tourism, then. How long do you plan to stay?"

She almost gave the wrong answer. "Until the war is over"

was definitely not what the official wanted to hear. "Two weeks, before I have to return to work."

"Enjoy your stay, Frau Hambach." He stamped her passport and handed it back to her.

The moment she held the precious document with the coveted entry stamp in her hand, all tension fell away from her. She had made it. She was in Switzerland; safe from persecution by the Nazis. She could hardly wait to send her mother the promised postcard.

After her, Bärbel was processed in the same perfunctory manner, whereas the official said to Felix: "Small border traffic as usual?"

"I'm picking up a few goods at Schöller's farm and will be back in an hour."

Astrid cast a surprised look at Felix. She had assumed he would immediately return to Sankt Gallenkirch.

About thirty meters past the second barrier, Felix stopped. The hardships of the last few days had etched themselves into his weather-beaten face. Finally, the tension dissolved, and he smiled. "Congratulations, you made it. That was by far the most adventurous tour I've ever done."

"I'm so happy!" Astrid wanted to jump up, shout, laugh, scream with joy—preferably all at once.

"I couldn't have imagined a better mountain guide than you. Thank you for taking me along." Bärbel looked as if tears were about to fall.

Felix seemed touched as well. His Adam's apple bobbed up and down several times before he answered: "You're welcome. It's nothing, really."

"On the contrary, you are a hero. Not everyone is as decent as you are." Bärbel furtively wiped a tear from her cheek. "My grandmother told me about the two Jewesses who were betrayed by one of the smugglers."

"That was Heinz," Felix grumbled.

Astrid felt the blood drain from her head. The landlady in Sankt Gallenkirch had recommended a smuggler named Heinz to her. It had to be the same man. Horrified, she whispered, "W-what happened to the women?"

Felix sighed. "They were hanged in the town square."

First her knees gave way, then fog appeared before Astrid's eyes. If Felix hadn't jumped to her aid and grabbed her under the arms, she would have tumbled to the ground.

"Hanged," she murmured, imagining the feel of the rope around her neck as it slowly but surely choked the life out of her. Fate had been kind to her. The friendly Bruno had prevented her from falling into the hands of an unscrupulous smuggler like Heinz.

"Are you all right?" Felix asked with concern.

"Yes. It must be the excitement." She didn't want to tell him the truth about her narrow escape. It was over. She never wanted to think of it again.

"I'll walk a little further with you toward the village. There you'll report to the police station. Explain to the officer on duty that you're politically persecuted, then he won't send you back. Political refugees receive asylum in Switzerland."

"The Swiss are sending Jews back to the German Reich?" Astrid's voice trembled with shock.

"Unfortunately, yes. I always urge Jews to push as far into the interior as possible. The further away from the border they're caught, the less likely they'll be expelled on the spot."

An icy hand pressed against Astrid's chest, causing her to gasp for air in panic. Without her mother's Aryan passport, the situation would look grim for her. In her thoughts, she whispered, "Thank you so much, Mutti."

About ten minutes later, Felix halted at a junction. "Well, you two, this is where our paths separate."

Bärbel stepped forward. "Are you sure the Gestapo won't be waiting for you once you return to Austria?"

"You can never know, but I don't think so." He shrugged.

"Thank you for everything you've done." Bärbel hugged him. "I'm deeply in your debt. How can I ever thank you enough?"

"That's not necessary." He pushed her away. "I'm glad you're both safe and sound."

Astrid shared Bärbel's emotion. "Without you, we would never have made it."

"Take care of yourselves! The war can't last much longer; better times will come once Hitler is defeated." With these words, he turned around and marched down a narrow path toward a farmstead.

"I hope he gets home safely," said Bärbel, speaking from Astrid's heart.

"I'm sure he will. He's as cunning as they come."

"Besides, he'll travel much faster without us. If they do stop him, he'll claim he was on a smuggling trip. That's probably the reason why he's visiting that farm."

Astrid's eyes widened. "I hadn't thought of that at all. He's organizing himself an alibi."

She took Bärbel's hand and together they walked down the path toward the village. After a while, she said, "My mother has a friend in Lucerne who's going to host me. Do you think I should mention this detail to the police?"

"Definitely. The authorities will be grateful if they can place you with someone instead of having to take care of you." Bärbel fell silent.

A few minutes later, Astrid addressed her: "What are your plans?"

"To be honest, I don't know. My escape wasn't planned. Since you sought shelter from the storm in the cave, events have been moving at breakneck speed. Now I suddenly find myself in Switzerland."

CHAPTER 27

After saying goodbye to Bärbel and Astrid, Felix marched toward the Schöller farm. It took longer than usual, because the past few days weighed heavy on his bones. He was happy about Guido's backpack, since it meant he wouldn't have to return home empty-handed. Schöller was one of his best suppliers.

Unlike in the German Reich, windows in neutral Switzerland glowed with light when darkness fell. They guided his way as night settled over the landscape around him.

Tired as a dog, he finally stepped into the farmyard. Someone must have seen him. Before he could knock on the door, it opened, and Josef Schöller stepped out.

"I was wondering where you've been. It's been quite a while since your last visit," the farmer grumbled.

"The weather threw a wrench in my plans." Although he had been doing business with Josef for many years, he had never told him about his side business of smuggling Jews. He intended to keep it that way despite harboring no illusions that the locals didn't know about the refugees crossing into their country. On the contrary, some were heavily involved in the business.

Besides, rumors spread quickly in this region, where everyone knew everyone else and half the population was related by marriage. However, they followed the old rule: What I don't know won't hurt me. Dealing with outsiders—and Felix definitely counted as an outsider even after decades of trading relations—one never discussed business other than one's own.

"Would you like to talk business first?" Josef asked.

Felix nodded, slightly surprised about the question. This was how they usually proceeded: money for goods, followed by a hearty soup in the kitchen and a glass of homemade schnapps. "Sure, why?"

"You look exhausted."

"I am." Felix considered how much of his odyssey to reveal. "I was caught off guard by a thunder storm and had to weather the night in a shelter along the way."

"The snow came early this year." The farmer led him to the barn. "If my rheumatism isn't mistaken, it is here to stay."

"I was afraid of that. Doesn't make the work any easier."

Josef slid the barn door open. "The usual? Coffee, sugar and chocolate."

"And tobacco, if you have any."

"It's gotten more expensive," Josef grumbled.

"Again? That's the third time this year." Felix was a master at the art of haggling.

"The blockade in the Mediterranean is giving us trouble. It's becoming increasingly difficult to buy good stuff from the Orient, not to mention Cuba."

"The Nazis lost the Atlantic Battle long ago," Felix protested.

"Supplies are practically impossible to get. I wouldn't

receive a thing, if it wasn't thanks to my good connections." Josef looked at him, the challenge lighting up his eyes. "You don't have to buy the tobacco. I have plenty of customers."

After they agreed on a price, Felix stowed the goods in Guido's backpack. He tucked two fine cigars in the outer pocket for the customs officers when he returned across the border later.

"Would you like a schnapps for the road?"

"Always, although I need a hearty soup more." Felix could do without the schnapps if necessary, but not without the warm meal. He had a good four-hour march ahead of him.

"You sure you want to head back tonight?" Josef looked up at the clear, black sky.

"The moon will be up soon. In the snow, it'll be bright enough." Felix had considered asking Josef for a place to sleep as he had often done in the past. But he'd been away much longer than planned and didn't want to leave Valentina worrying about him another night.

"If you say so." In the hallway, they removed their dirty mountain boots. Every visitor had to put on felt slippers before entering the living room—Josef's wife ran a strict regimen.

At the large dining table sat two men whom Felix recognized as the woodcutter Hans and the farmer Martin. They were spooning soup from a bowl in the middle of the table.

"*Gruezi,*" they greeted him, smacking their lips.

Felix sat down on an empty chair and waited until Josef's wife waltzed in to give him a spoon. The men ate in silence until the bowl was empty, then they broke off pieces of bread and soaked up the remaining soup. No food shortage existed in Switzerland like it did in the war-ravaged Third Reich; however, people didn't let food go to waste either.

"That was good." Martin wiped his mouth with the back of his hand.

Josef leaned back, folding his hands over his considerable paunch. "Would you like some schnapps?"

The three guests nodded, and Josef called out, "Hey, woman, bring us a bottle of the good stuff and four glasses."

Shortly afterward, the farmer's wife appeared. Casting her husband a disapproving look, she placed the requested items in front of him. "Remember that you have to go down to the valley in the morning."

"I could drive that road blindfolded, so stop nagging."

She pursed her lips and left the room in direction of the kitchen. Josef let out an audible sigh. "Never get married, or you'll be bossed around day in and day out."

Felix remained silent. He had no intention of interfering in the Schöllers' marriage. Besides, Josef didn't need to know that Valentina, though not Felix's wife, still bossed him around constantly. Especially his trips to the tavern were a thorn in her side. Women simply didn't understand what men needed.

"Have you heard?" Josef pushed a full glass to each of them. "Over by Gargellen, they shot a Jew who was trying to escape."

So the news about poor Bruno had already made the rounds. If there was one thing one could rely on, it was the rumor mill. Felix downed his shot in one gulp. The schnapps burned down his throat into his stomach, leaving a pleasant warmth. "That's news to me."

"Come on," Hans growled. "The entire region is talking about nothing else. The wildest stories are circulating."

"I've been on the road for a few days. Haven't met anyone." Felix tried to extricate himself.

"They found the smuggler's backpack." Martin glared at

him, apparently hoping to evoke a reaction, while at the same time holding out his empty glass to Josef for a refill.

"I have mine with me. It's in the hallway next to my boots."

"Supposedly there was a woman with them too."

Again, Felix feigned ignorance. "Do they know what happened to her?"

"She's still missing. The Germans don't have her. Therefore our foreign police are sniffing around," Josef chimed in. "As if we had nothing better to do than hide foreigners."

"If I happen to meet the woman, I'll let you know." In retrospect, Felix was glad he had taken Bärbel with him, since two women traveling together looked far less suspicious than a lone woman already being hunted by the police on both sides of the border.

Hans, the woodcutter, snorted with contempt. "Don't act so sanctimonious. Everyone here knows you've got dirt on your hands."

"If by dirt you mean sugar, tobacco and chocolate, I definitely agree." Felix shrugged. "I have nothing to do with the missing companion of a dead Jew. I stay far away from such business. Much too risky."

Josef refilled the shots once more. "Come on. You know Felix is as silent as the grave. You won't worm anything out of him."

"It would be downright suicidal for me to come here if I in fact had anything to do with the missing person, wouldn't it?"

Martin rubbed his dark beard. "Maybe. Or maybe not. Doesn't really matter anyway. Soon the Nazis will be history."

"I'll drink to that," said Felix.

"Those bastards are constantly causing problems. Last

week they paid me half the agreed price for my timber delivery. My contribution to the final victory, they said."

"The final victory," Josef scoffed. "As if Germany could still win the war. They're so close to being annihilated." He put his forefinger and thumb about half an inch from each other to demonstrate just how close.

"They can fight for a long time. But whatever, as long as the Nazi bigwigs hide their money at our banks, nothing will happen to us."

The more the schnapps flowed, the more the three men lapsed into their Swiss-German dialect, which Felix had difficulties understanding. The strain of the last few days took its toll. Satiated and warm, he leaned against the back of his chair.

"Isn't that right, Felix?" Martin's voice jolted him from his dreams.

Despite not knowing what they were talking about, he answered, "I think so." In the next second, his head dropped to his chest as sleep overcame him. A rough nudge woke him up.

Martin had risen from his chair, swaying heavily. "I'd better go now. Or my old lady will raise hell."

"I'll come with you." Hans, too, had trouble getting upright. Clinging to each other, they swayed into the hallway, where they needed several minutes to tie their bootlaces. Then the door slammed shut after them.

The cold gust of air sobered Felix. Glancing at the wall clock, he was shocked to realize it was shortly before midnight. He jumped up in one bounce.

Josef placed a paw on his shoulder and said with glassy eyes, "You'd better stay here."

"We have a full moon," Felix protested.

"Don't be stupid. You don't have a wife who'll make your

life hell if you stay away overnight. There's no need to descend in the dark."

Felix was dead tired, so it didn't take much persuasion to change his mind. "I'll stay. Thanks for the offer."

"You know where." Josef turned away and stumbled up the stairs to his bedroom while Felix walked across the yard and threw himself onto the cot in a chamber next to the stable. Just before he dozed off, the thought of his sister crossed his mind. He inwardly shrugged, since she must have gone to bed hours ago and was probably sound asleep. She wouldn't even notice whether he came home tonight or not.

The next morning, after a hearty breakfast of milk, cheese, bacon, fried eggs and freshly baked bread, Felix set off. The raising sun gilded the mountain peaks, and the frozen snow crunched beneath his boots.

Up at the pass, the Swiss officials waved him through without leaving their warm shelter. On the German side, however, he was stopped at the barrier. He knew the two border guards well. Like almost everyone who served up here, they weren't averse to a small token of appreciation for swift processing.

Unlike Meinhold and Christoph though, these two were staunch Nazis who would never let a Jew slip through the net.

"Where are you headed?" one asked.

"Home to Sankt Gallenkirch. I was held up at the Schöller farm. Had wanted to return yesterday evening." The customs officers didn't like it when a local in small border traffic stayed overnight.

"Too much schnapps?"

Felix nodded and rummaged in his backpack for the Cuban cigars. "The Schöller's homemade brew is not for weak men. He sends his regards."

The border guard whistled through his teeth. "Genuine

Havanas? Haven't smoked one in a long time." He lit the cigar immediately. A spicy aroma wafted into Felix's nostrils.

"Until next time." The colleague opened the barrier.

Felix marched at a brisk speed toward the farm where Valentina must be frantic with sorrow due to his prolonged absence. Inwardly, he prepared himself for a vicious scolding and his sister's inevitable whining that he should end the Jewish tours.

Despite being tempted to comply with her request after this hellish experience, he knew he would help again as soon as Karl showed up with someone who needed to flee the Nazis. Just as Guido had done. The pitcher goes to the well until it breaks. Nothing could change that.

After a good three hours of marching, he reached a hill from which he could see the Wallner farm. The homey feeling vanished the moment he noticed smoke rising from the chimney next to the house.

Felix stood rooted to the spot. They had agreed to use that chimney in case of imminent danger. Something terrible must have happened. He ignored the urge to sprint down and make sure his family was safe. No matter how much he wanted to, they had decided that he wouldn't come home when she lit that chimney.

After recovering from the initial shock, he pulled the hand mirror from the backpack. Catching sunbeams, he directed the light at the kitchen window, behind which Valentina should be busy preparing lunch at this hour.

Short - short - long - short. Pause. Short - long - long. He signaled his initials, F and W, in Morse code. This way Valentina knew he had received her warning. Now he had to wait for her answer. Minutes stretched into eternity as he waited. Nothing stirred in the house. He began to fear for the worst.

He signaled a second time.

Finally the response came: three short, two long. The number three. Felix took a deep breath. He and Valentina had established three emergency hideouts, number three was in the dilapidated watchtower. That was where she wanted to meet him. He signaled his agreement. The hike to the tower took about twenty minutes. There he sat down and waited for his sister, the uncertainty gnawing at his insides.

CHAPTER 28

"We should make our way directly to Lucerne," Astrid suddenly said as they walked down the snow-covered path into the valley, "without reporting to the police here."

Bärbel stopped. "But Felix said ..."

"I don't want to be stuck in some camp. My mother's friend will help us. She knows many important people."

"Us?" Bärbel was uncomfortable that Astrid was including her in the venture so naturally. "I don't know this woman. I'm a stranger to her."

"You're not a stranger. You saved my life. Without you, I would never have survived those terrible days. I would have died somewhere out there on the mountain." A shudder shook Astrid's shoulders. "Shot like poor Bruno. Or crushed by an avalanche. Or..." Astrid's voice broke.

"I just did what had to be done." Bärbel didn't feel like a heroine. Helping the other woman had been a matter of course for her.

"Still, I'm in your debt. Come with me. Please. It's the least I can do to show my gratitude."

The sincere warmth in Astrid's voice touched Bärbel deeply. "Thank you, but I can't accept the offer. It's very generous of this friend to take you in. You can't expect her to feed another person."

"I'm sure she wouldn't mind."

"That's really sweet of you. But you don't have to worry about me, I'll be fine."

"Where do you want to go?"

"First to the police station in the valley, like Felix suggested. I'm sure they'll tell me what will be happening to me and where they're sending me." Bärbel didn't want to impose on Astrid's Swiss acquaintance, but at the same time she was reluctant to let Astrid travel to Lucerne alone. Who knew what dangers she might encounter on the way? So she made one more attempt. "Why don't you come with me to the police? Tell the officers about your friend. I'm sure they'll send you to her, since they would be happy to have a fugitive taken off their hands."

Astrid looked down, silent for a moment, before she whispered: "Or they'll deport me."

"Felix said himself that political refugees aren't deported. It's only they Jews they don't want in Switzerland." Bärbel remembered his words.

Astrid whispered. "I told you I'm half Jewish."

"That's right." In the exuberance of joy at finally being safe, she had forgotten this detail. She racked her brain. "You showed the border guard an Aryan passport. Nobody knows about your origins."

"The passport belongs to my mother. She gave it to me so that I could flee abroad, since the Gestapo summoned me."

"I remember you mentioned that. The thing with the yellow star."

"At least that's what the summons said. But maybe someone saw me picking the lock of the Gestapo warehouses and snitched on me." Astrid raised her eyebrows in a silent plea.

"You committed a burglary?" A cold shiver ran through Bärbel's veins. No wonder the padlock in the tunnel hadn't posed a problem for Astrid.

"Yes and no." Astrid sighed. "During a house search, the Gestapo confiscated our electric stove. We absolutely had to have it back, otherwise we would have starved to death."

"Stealing isn't a solution. Couldn't you have eaten cold food?" As usual, Bärbel thought practically. "After all, a hearty snack fills you up too."

"We were out of bread. The officers even spilled the flour on the floor and trampled on it with their dirty boots."

Bärbel's eyes widened in horror. "But ... that's ... criminal."

"Welcome to my world," said Astrid.

After a moment of shock, Bärbel asked, "Did they really want to starve you to death?"

"Who knows for sure? As a Jew, you always stand with one foot in the grave. The Gestapo can do whatever they want, and no one will bring them to justice. How many of my friends do you think have disappeared never to be seen again?" Astrid talked herself into a rage. "Deported and never heard from again, committed suicide in prison, allegedly shot on the run ... and those who returned from a concentration camp are mere empty shells of their former selves, broken, destroyed. Walking corpses."

"I can't believe that."

Astrid shook her head with a sad expression. "You have no idea what it's like to live as a Jew in the German Reich."

"Apparently I really don't have that perspective. I don't personally know anyone who is Jewish."

"See? The Nazis have succeeded in their goal. Since Hitler came to power, they have harassed, expelled and isolated us. It was a perfidious plan, which unfortunately worked brilliantly. Because most people fight against injustice only when it affects them or their friends and relatives. Hardly anyone risks their life for strangers."

Bärbel swallowed the guilt. She had blamed the Nazis for the criminal war, had been upset about cruelty and injustice, yet she hadn't started actively resisting until she met Christoph. "I am sorry. I felt bullied by the Nazis, but it turns out that my life was privileged despite everything."

"Don't be sorry." Astrid smiled. "Most people in Germany don't really know how we Jews are doing. After all, we were excluded from society years ago, forced into Jewish houses, and banned from public life. We hardly appear at all anymore. The only people who still stick by our family are my mother's Aryan relatives. Even they do it secretly because they're afraid for their own lives."

The shock seeped deep into Bärbel's soul. She wished she had realized this years ago. Then she would have done more. Or at least she would have done something at all.

"I'm so sorry," Bärbel repeated. "I didn't know." During their conversation, Bärbel and Astrid had continued walking. They approached the village in silence.

"I can't take the risk of being deported." Astrid's voice was toneless.

"If you don't tell them, how are they going to find out that you're half-Jewish?"

"My mother's passport is genuine. The date of birth isn't. It won't stand up to a thorough check. Once they get suspicious, it will be easy to find out my true identity." Astrid paused. "My best chance is to go and see Marie Steiner in Lucerne. She's well connected. She'll find a way for me to stay. If she vouches for me, the immigration police won't even consider investigating my case."

Bärbel was torn between the need to report legally to the local police station and the need to stand by Astrid. At some point, she looked Astrid in the eye. "How are you going to make your way to Lucerne? You don't have any Swiss francs."

"I still have my mother's gold ring." Astrid pushed her lower lip forward in defiance. "If I pawn it in the next town, I'll have enough money for a ticket to Lucerne."

"And you think you can just walk into a store like that without causing a stir? A stranger who doesn't even understand the local dialect?"

Gradually, Astrid seemed to realize how reckless her plan was. A slight tremor drowned out the firmness of her voice. "I have to take this risk. If I fall into the hands of the Gestapo, I'm as good as dead."

Bärbel wrestled with herself until she threw all caution to the wind. "All right. I'll come with you to the next bigger town. I'll make the ring into money for you there, but after that we'll part ways."

"Thanks a million." Astrid seemed to grow a few centimeters. "To tell you the truth, I'm afraid to continue the journey alone."

They set off again. Exhausted from the strenuous day, their progress was slow. Meanwhile it had turned dark, and the lights of the village showed them the way. As they passed a brightly lit farmhouse, Bärbel suggested, "Let's ask if we can spend the night here."

Startled, Astrid shook her head. "I'd rather not."

"What else are you going to do? We'll have to sleep sometime. It's more dangerous in the village, right next to the police station."

Astrid frowned until she finally nodded. "Fine, but what should we say?"

"The truth," Bärbel grinned, "at least half the truth: that we were on our way to the village, were surprised by the darkness and got lost."

"If you say so." Astrid didn't seem convinced by the idea.

Bärbel implored her, "It's the best solution. The farmers won't want to leave the house this late. Especially not into the village to report two exhausted hikers to the police."

"At the first sign that something is going wrong, I'll run."

"And I'll stop the pursuers." Bärbel didn't think it would come to that. On the contrary, she was hoping for some hot soup and a place to sleep. After this terrible day, she was in desperate need of both.

"I want your sense of humor," Astrid grumbled, the hint of a smile finally flitting across her face. "Let's look on the bright side: it can't get much worse than what we've been through in the last few days. People have been shot, we've hidden in a hole beneath the ground, crawled through a tunnel to freedom and almost got buried under an avalanche. What else could possibly go wrong?"

"Shh. Don't jinx it!" Bärbel covered her ears. "You mustn't tempt fate."

"You're not superstitious, are you?" Astrid started laughing out loud. "I thought you were studying medicine? Isn't that a science?"

"Not an exact one like mathematics. There are many things in medicine which we can't explain. Some people die of polio, others survive it. So far, no one has found out what exactly enables some people to beat the virus, while the rest are scarred for life if they don't die."

Astrid raised her hands defensively. "Thank you, I understand. I won't say any more."

Then they marched along the driveway to the farmhouse. When they knocked, the farmer's wife initially received them with a gruff demeanor, but relented and took the two strangers in for the night, even serving them a hearty soup and homemade bread.

As she led Bärbel and Astrid into a room next to the

stable, she gave them directions to the village and told them to leave before breakfast.

"See? That went well," said Bärbel before the exertions of the day took their toll and she fell asleep in a matter of seconds.

CHAPTER 29

Felix didn't have to wait long until Valentina rushed up to his hiding place.

"Are you all right?" Felix jumped up.

"I am." She was just slightly out of breath, even though she had covered the distance in record time in addition to carrying a large backpack. "What about you?"

Suspicious that she didn't scold him straight away, he narrowed his eyes. "I had to weather a thunderstorm and was caught by the onset of winter."

"You were outrageously lucky." Something was very wrong here. Under normal circumstances his sister would be lamenting how worried she was about him because he had been away for far too long.

"That's all? You're not ranting?" he challenged her.

"What use will it be?" She walked past him into the interior of the dilapidated tower. "Give me a hand with the backpack."

It was much heavier than it looked. As he took the luggage off her back, Felix all but dropped to his knees. "What have you got in there? Bricks?"

"Tins of canned food."

A bad feeling snaked up his spine. First she didn't tell him off for being late, next the heavy luggage ... "Are you going to tell me what's happening? Why did you send me a warning?"

"They've arrested Karl."

Felix's stomach tightened. Karl knew everyone and everything. He wasn't just Felix's business partner, he was a central part of a huge network of helpers in the hinterland: counterfeiters, church representatives, politicians, and escape helpers in Switzerland who worked together to snatch Jews away from Nazi persecution.

Karl could arrange for anything one's heart desired. He supplied wealthy Nazis with luxury goods such as coffee and sugar, who in turn showed their gratitude by providing blank official forms or other favors. For refugees, he procured ration cards, clothing cards, false IDs, money... simply everything. Without Karl, the network was deprived of its most important pillar. He was also Felix's best friend.

"When?" he asked.

"It was probably a few days ago, but we don't know exactly." Valentina paused. "The Gestapo tortured him."

That was to be expected, yet the confirmation gave Felix another punch in the gut. Not only because he felt pity for his friend, but also because he himself was in mortal danger if Karl had spilled the beans. They had been working together for years; Karl could accuse him of so many crimes that it was enough for a hundred convictions.

"Don't worry." Valentina, who usually wasn't squeamish, pulled her face into a disgusted grimace. "He bit off his tongue so he couldn't tell them anything."

The image in his head made Felix retch several times. "If I catch the pigs, I'll skin them alive!"

"You won't do anything," Valentina replied forcefully. "You're not allowed to come home. This morning the Gestapo came to ask about you. Someone saw you with two strangers. The Gestapo are convinced one of them was the Viennese Jew who was shot."

"What did you tell them?" Felix had feared he might be linked to Bruno. The Gestapo weren't stupid, and it would have been a huge coincidence for him to go on tour at the same time, without being involved in the escape of the two Jewish fugitives.

"I stated truthfully that you had gone on tour and that I expected you back any day." Her eyes flashed. "Before I added that you're a miserable jerk and they'll probably find you drunk in the pub."

"Does that mean they haven't found my backpack?" After the stories he had heard at the Schöller farm, Felix could have sworn the police had by now identified who the luggage belonged to.

"They have. But because they haven't found your body, they assume you've made a run for it." She shook her head. "What were you thinking?"

Felix ignored her remark. "Nothing will happen to you and the children as long as the Gestapo don't find me."

A mischievous grin finally spread across her cheeks. "The twins were relieved of their anti-aircraft duty effective immediately due to political unreliability."

"It seems the misery has done some good after all." At home in the mountains on the Wallner farm, far away from the war theater, the boys were better placed than in the city as anti-aircraft helpers.

"The police turned the house upside down." Valentina rolled her eyes in disgust. "You can't imagine how much dirt and chaos they've left behind. It will take me days to clean everything up."

"Did they find anything?" Starting in his early childhood, Felix's father had drilled it into them not to keep compromising documents. He never wrote anything down the police could use against him. If it was unavoidable, he wrote down names and addresses in a notebook, the pages of which he tore out and destroyed as soon as the action was over.

"Nothing of importance. Their boss took a box of cigars as evidence."

"Shit, I wanted to put them in the stash."

"No big deal, you'll get a few days in jail for a box of cigars." She looked at him sternly. "Before you get any ideas, this time it's serious. You mustn't show your face in the village, otherwise they'll book you for helping those Viennese Jews to escape. Plus obstructing state authority, illegally crossing the border and whatever else they can come up with. The escape aid alone is enough to get you hanged."

"Thanks, I'd rather not take my chances." Felix pointed to the bulging backpack. "What's in there?"

"Clothes, food, an ice axe, crampons, a flashlight, a radio, spare batteries, everything you need to spend the winter in the mountains."

"You've thought of everything."

"I want you to survive." She squeezed his hand. "Miserable jerk or not. You're my brother and I love you."

Moved, he put an arm around her shoulder. "I hate to leave you alone on the farm."

"The twins are back. Besides, you were on tour most of the time anyway."

"I know, and I'm sorry. I didn't mean to cause you grief. But you have to understand that I couldn't stand by idly, watching the Nazis wipe out entire parts of our population."

She pulled away from his embrace. "Take care of yourself. Send me a message via the young shepherd if you need anything."

Felix slapped his forehead with the flat of his hand. "I

completely forgot. Old Guido is dead. Shot by the Nazis. His dog too."

Valentina's eyes widened. "He certainly didn't deserve such an end."

"Guido was old and tired of life. But he must have wished for a more peaceful death." Felix wondered whether he should tell her about the avalanche. To avoid giving his sister any more bad news, he decided not to. She had enough to deal with.

"Take care of yourself. Once a week I'll bring more food to one of our hiding places. If it's gone when I visit next, I'll know you're still alive."

"Perhaps I'll stay in Switzerland for the winter. I'm sure I could find somewhere to work."

"No." She shook her head in horror. "Christoph told me the border guards received instructions this morning to arrest you if you show up."

"Thanks for the warning. Now leave, so no one notices your absence." After removing what he needed of Guido's things, he switched backpacks with her.

"I'll talk to you in the spring. And don't you dare die until then!"

After a quick embrace Valentina marched off. He stared at her figure until he lost sight of her, shouldered the backpack and set off. He would manage. After all, he knew the region like the back of his hand.

CHAPTER 30

Golden leaves littered the cobblestones of Lucerne, the trees along the lake standing bare against a gray autumn sky. Astrid had almost given up hope when, after weeks of waiting, a letter finally arrived.

It was addressed to Marie Steiner, who handed it to Astrid with the words, "I'm sure the letter is meant for you. Your mother merely addressed it to me because of the censorship."

Astrid reverently took the envelope in her hand, which was her only connection to her family. She imagined smelling her mother's scent and pressed the letter to her heart before opening it.

My dearest Marie,

How pleased I was to hear from you. It is admirable that you walk along the lake to feed the ducks in these temperatures. It makes me happy to know you have so much joy in your life.

Not much has changed with us, the family is healthy and well. So don't worry about me. I'll be fine. The neighbors help each other wherever they can. Frau Berger sometimes gives us some of her potatoes, and I stuff her stockings in return. She's really not very good at it.

Astrid had to smile. Frau Berger lived in a mixed marriage like her mother. Unlike Mother though, she didn't have two constantly hungry sons to look after, just herself and her husband, who was fed relatively generously at his workplace.

Frau Rosenthal died after a long illness. Shortly afterward, her husband and son moved out. They are said to have found a better apartment outside Frankfurt.

Astrid's hand with the letter sank to her lap as a cold shiver racked her shoulders. A better apartment outside probably meant they had been deported to Theresienstadt.

In Jewish circles, deportation to Theresienstadt was considered a privilege, since it was regarded as the least terrible camp in the East, offering higher chances of survival. Either way, old Herr Rosenthal wouldn't last long. According to the coded postcards some inmates had managed to send, the terrible conditions in the camp, rife with illnesses, were already killing hundreds. At least his half-Jewish son, young and strong, had a chance of surviving the camp.

I'm sure you've heard about the British bombing campaign. We won't let this get us down. On the contrary, these war crimes bring us Germans closer together. It can't be long now until the war is over.

I hope we can meet again then, dear Marie. I was so pleased to hear that you are no longer living alone, but have found a young girl to help you. Despite not knowing her, I'm sure she'll be good company to you. Give her my best regards.

A warm hug,
Sieglinde

Marie, who had tactfully left her alone, returned to the living room two cups of real coffee in her hands and sat down next to Astrid. "What does your mother write?"

"Not much." Astrid folded the letter carefully. "You have

to read between the lines. They are managing, despite the situation getting more difficult by the day. She sends you her warmest regards and thanks you for taking me in so generously."

"That goes without saying." Marie handed her a cup. "I pray every day that your family survives the war."

"Me too," Astrid murmured. "Sometimes I feel guilty living with you like a maggot in bacon while Mutti has to beg the neighbor for potatoes."

"There's no reason to feel guilty. Sieglinde sent you away so you wouldn't get arrested."

"I know." Astrid sighed.

"If it makes you feel better, I'll let you starve on dry bread and water," Marie suggested with a wink.

Astrid erupted into laughter. "No thanks, that won't be necessary."

Her thoughts wandered to Bärbel, who lived in a refugee camp on the outskirts of the city. Despite Astrid's attempts at persuasion, she had refused to be a burden on Marie Steiner and had chosen to be admitted to the camp, where she had to stay until the war ended.

It hadn't taken the energetic woman long to convince the head of the infirmary to allow her to help on a voluntary basis. Switzerland did not suffer the same shortage of doctors as the German Reich did, yet there was always a need for a capable medical student.

Astrid regularly met up with her for a coffee and a Schoggiweggli—a yeast pastry filled with chocolate. They had pleasant chats, which reminded both of them how lucky they had been to escape the Nazis.

They hadn't heard anything about Felix. Sometimes, when Astrid lay awake at night, she saw his weather-beaten face in front of her, heard his calm voice encouraging her. She remembered his determination to get his charges across the border to safety against all odds.

Having him as her mountain guide, she had always been certain that they would somehow make it. Every time she thought of him, she hoped that he had survived the adventure and had returned back home to Sankt Gallenkirch, where he was guiding other refugees on their perilous journey to freedom.

"The war can't last much longer." Marie's words snapped her out of her thoughts.

"Mutti wrote that too." Every day, Astrid vacillated between hope and despair, depending on which newspaper she was reading. The German editions of English newspapers gave her hope, while *Das Reich*, written by Goebbels' propaganda ministry, made it seem as if Germany was on the verge of victory.

"The Germans are losing on all fronts. The Italians have surrendered, the Russians are advancing from the east."

Astrid nodded. She had learned to be cautious with her hopes, since she had been disappointed too many times.

She finished her coffee, carried the dishes to the sink, and looked out of the window at the peaceful city. Lucerne sometimes seemed like a fairy tale to her: no rubble or ruins, no half-starved people, no one wearing the yellow star while scurrying through the streets with their eyes downcast. But she wouldn't be truly happy until her family had survived Hitler's regime.

LETTER FROM THE AUTHOR

Thank you for reading **Perilous Journey to Freedom**. If you enjoyed the book, I would appreciate receiving a short or long review.

If you want to be the first to know when a new book is published, sign up for my newsletter:
https://kummerow.info

The idea for this book entered my mind on a hike in the Austrian Alps. There are numerous stories recounting an escape across the Pyrenees using one of the so-called "Escape Lines". But I hadn't read anything about an escape across the Alps, yet I was sure someone had done it.

Doing research I found out about Meinrad Juen, a professional smuggler from Sankt Gallenkirch in Montafon, who smuggled Jews and other persecuted people across the border into Switzerland starting in 1938.

He was widely known in the region, a man who didn't care about conventions and who stood by his opinions. It is rumored he was one of two people in the village voting against the annexation of Austria to the German Reich.

LETTER FROM THE AUTHOR

For years, he and his brother Wilhelm Juen smuggled escapees across the border in groups of up to seven people. In real life, unlike in my novel, Meinrad Juen was arrested in October 1942. The reason was never known, apparently his name and address was found during a search of the house of a Viennese Jew, who had been planning to escape.

The policeman who was tasked with transferring Meinrad Juen to the prison in the nearby town of Schruns was also a good customer. Therefore he allowed Meinrad to visit his sister Ludwina to say goodbye. At her farm, Meinrad took the opportunity to escape. He went into hiding and lived in various places with relatives and acquaintances until the end of the war.

He died of a heart attack in 1949 at the age of 63. His brother Wilhelm lived in Sankt Gallenkirch until 1974.

The fictional Felix was named after my mountain guide on the above-mentioned hike through the Austrian Alps, who impressed me greatly with his care and concern for the group.

Besides the Montafon, there were other regions where people from the German Reich were smuggled into Switzerland. As I mentioned in the last book of the series, most of them tried their luck via the Rhine Valley, but as time progressed, this route became better guarded.

For better or worse, the fugitives therefore attempted the more difficult route over the mountains, which was impossible without local guides.

The website https://www.ueber-die-grenze.at/ has an interesting collection of escape stories taking place on the Austrian-Swiss border from Bregenz at Lake Constance to the Silvretta in the south.

Along cycle route no. 1, there are a total of 52 audio stations narrating the escape stories described on the website. If you are ever in the area, it's certainly worth a detour to listen to a few of them.

LETTER FROM THE AUTHOR

You probably know that the White Rose group was mainly active in Munich. However, some of the students had family in nearby cities such as Ulm or Augsburg, taking leaflets with them on family visits and distributing them in those cities.

In the Ludwig Maximilian University in Munich, in the very atrium where Sophie and Hans Scholl were arrested, there is a very interesting exhibition about the activities of the White Rose.

Nonetheless, it was purely by chance that I found out Christoph Probst had been transferred to Innsbruck University in the fall of 1942, where the fictional Bärbel was studying. What would be more obvious than letting the two become acquainted? Her involvement in the resistance provided a good reason why Bärbel had to flee in a hurry.

Astrid Hambach's experiences during the house search are not an invention on my part. Viktor Klemperer, a German literary professor and a Jew described similar scenes in his diaries "I want to bear witness".

In Dresden, where he lived in a mixed marriage, there seem to have been countless house searches, especially in the years 1941-43. He aptly describes the daily fear of whether it would happen again that day.

Depending on the mood of the officials, a house search could end badly for those affected. Not only were food and furniture destroyed, but the residents were often beaten hard enough to need hospitalization.

I also learned about Bärbel's ignorance of the Jewish living conditions from Viktor Klemperer. In his diaries, he regularly complains that even good friends who send them food have no idea how bad the situation actually is.

I have already written extensively about Switzerland's attitude toward Jewish refugees in the last book, **Dark Shadows Looming Ahead**.

LETTER FROM THE AUTHOR

At the repeated request of my readers, the next book is about an old acquaintance: Roxy from the Berlin Wife series. The new book features her story, as well as the persecution of Sinti and Roma, before she meets David.

Yours sincerely,
    Marion Kummerow

ALSO BY MARION KUMMEROW

Love and Resistance in WW2 Germany

Unrelenting

Unyielding

Unwavering

War Girl Series

Downed over Germany (Prequel)

Blonde Angel: War Girl Ursula (Book 1)

War Girl Lotte (Book 2)

War Girl Anna (Book 3)

Reluctant Informer (Book 4)

Trouble Brewing (Book 5)

Fatal Encounter (Book 6)

Uncommon Sacrifice (Book 7)

Bitter Tears (Book 8)

Secrets Revealed (Book 9)

Together at Last (Book 10)

Endless Ordeal (Book 11)

Not Without My Sister (Spin-off)

Second Chance at First Love (romantic spin-off)

Berlin Fractured

From the Ashes (Book 1)

On the Brink (Book 2)

In the Skies (Book 3)
Into the Unknown (Book 4)
Against the Odds (Book 5)

Margarete's Story

Turning Point (Prequel)
A Light in the Window
From the Dark We Rise
The Girl in the Shadows
Daughter of the Dawn

Standalone

The Orphan's Mother

German Wives

The Berlin Wife
The Berlin Wife's Choice
The Berlin Wife's Resistance
The Berlin Wife's Vow

Escaping the Reich

Three Children in Danger
Dark Shadows Looming Ahead
Perilous Journey to Freedom

Find all my books here:
http://www.kummerow.info

CONTACT ME

I truly appreciate you taking the time to read (and enjoy) my books. And I'd be thrilled to hear from you!
If you'd like to get in touch with me you can do so via

Facebook:
http://www.facebook.com/AutorinKummerow

Website
http://www.kummerow.info